"Before I leave...I'll give you the sweetest revenge of all."

Nick continued, "I still want you, Barbie Lamb." His fingers stroked slowly up her cheeks. "Is that sweet to hear?"

Her heart was pounding so hard she couldn't think. Couldn't move, either.

"Let me make it even sweeter for you. Much better to taste the wanting, feel the wanting."

His head was bending and she knew he was going to kiss her. The sizzle of challenge was in his eyes, heating her blood, stirring needs she couldn't repress, memories of how it had been together....

Australian author **EMMA DARCY** has written more than seventy novels, including the international bestseller *The Secrets Within*, published by MIRA® Books. Her intense, passionate and fast-paced writing style has made Emma Darcy popular with readers around the world, and she's sold nearly 60 million copies of her books worldwide.

Coming soon in Presents Passion™
The Hot-Blooded Groom #2195
on sale August 2001

Books by Emma Darcy

HARLEQUIN PRESENTS®
2110—THE CATTLE KING'S MISTRESS*
2116—THE PLAYBOY KING'S WIFE*
2122—THE PLEASURE KING'S BRIDE*
2157—THE MARRIAGE RISK

*Kings of the Outback trilogy

Emma Darcy

THE SWEETEST REVENGE

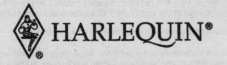

HARLEQUIN®

TORONTO • NEW YORK • LONDON
AMSTERDAM • PARIS • SYDNEY • HAMBURG
STOCKHOLM • ATHENS • TOKYO • MILAN • MADRID
PRAGUE • WARSAW • BUDAPEST • AUCKLAND

ISBN 0-373-12176-8

THE SWEETEST REVENGE

First North American Publication 2001.

Copyright © 2001 by Emma Darcy.

This edition published by arrangement with Harlequin Books S.A.

Visit us at www.eHarlequin.com

Printed in U.S.A.

CHAPTER ONE

MONDAY morning, and as usual, the staff of Multi-Media Promotions was abuzz with the swapping of weekend news before everyone settled down to work. Nick Armstrong exchanged only brief greetings as he strode to his private office, trailed by his friend and business partner, Leon Webster. The moment his door was shut, he released his pent-up anger to the one person who *should* understand his situation.

'You know what Tanya said to me on Saturday, after I'd called off our planned outing *once again?*' he exploded.

'Something undoubtedly designed to cut you off at the knees,' came the voice of experience.

Nick grimaced, remembering that Leon had just been through a nasty break-up with a live-in girl-friend. 'She said what I really wanted was a toy doll whose feelings wouldn't be hurt from being left on a shelf until I had time for playing.'

'Sounds good! A toy doll wouldn't nag.'

'Better still, a fairy princess doll...'

'Yep. Beautiful, glamorous, long blond hair, sparkling eyes, a smile to warm a man's heart...'

'...with a magic wand that would give me the energy to be the kind of lover that even a plastic toy would expect of a man.'

'Oooh... we're getting into kinky stuff here.'

'Leon, this is serious. And we are going to have a serious discussion.'

Eyebrows lifted mockingly. 'About women?'

'About business.' Nick glowered at his friend as he rounded the desk and dropped into his chair. 'Take a seat. And wipe that smirk off your face. This is deadly serious.'

'The man is wounded,' Leon muttered, settling into a chair with a mournful expression. Seeing Nick's irritation, he made an effort to present a suitably serious countenance.

It was dangerous to rile Nick in this mood. He was the darkly brooding type—a creative genius and a computer whiz from way back—and he often needed lightening up, but this was not the moment, Leon decided.

They were opposites in many ways. Even in looks. Nick—tall, black-haired, blue-eyed, had a face and body that were stamped with masculine strength, both physical and mental. Oddly enough, Leon never felt diminished by him. While he himself was only average height and his colouring wasn't so dramatic, having fairish brown hair and brown eyes, he had the gift of the gab and could attract any woman he wanted.

They made a great team—the design king and the salesman—and Leon was not about to allow anything to disturb it. Besides which, his partner's mental well-being was of paramount importance to their success.

'Business!' Nick tapped the desk with a strong index finger for emphasis. 'You know how much the Internet stuff has taken off, Leon. I'm snowed under. I need two more graphic designers to help take the load.'

'That will cut into our profits,' he cautioned.

'I need a life, too,' Nick bit out.

Leon rolled his eyes. 'Just because Tanya got in a snit over not getting your undivided attention? She doesn't own you, Nick, and take it from me...'

Blue lightning flashed straight back at him. 'I take a lot from you, Leon. You're a fantastic salesman and we're doing great, but I will not work to this pressure anymore.'

Hands instantly lifted into a truce position. 'Okay, okay,' he soothed. 'So long as this is *you* talking and not Tanya. You always said if we worked like dogs until we're thirty...'

'I'm thirty next week. Both of us pocketed over five million dollars last year...'

'And may well pocket twice that this year.'

'But we've paid a price for it. You lost Liz...'

'There you go, bringing women into it...'

'Damn it, Leon! I want a life beyond work, even if you don't. I'm thirty next week. Enough's enough. I need more staff.'

'Okay, okay. I'll ask around. Head-hunt someone good for you.'

Nick held up two fingers.

Leon sighed. Two more salaries to pay. 'So we'll get someone good and one out of design school to be trained. How's that?'

'Cheapskate.'

'Not at all. Common sense to train them our way. You know that, Nick.'

Nick privately conceded the point, but was not about to relax his stance on the issue. 'Get right onto it, Leon. And don't be giving me any delay tactics. I don't care what it costs. It will cost a damned sight more if I reach burnout.'

'Don't mention that word!' Horror-struck, Leon jackknifed from his chair. 'Your wish is my command, dear boy. I shall go forth this moment and head-hunt.'

'A trainee, as well.'

'No problem. They'll be storming the portals to get in here.' He strode to the door and paused, looking back with cynical eyes. 'I bet Tanya is still coming to your birthday bash. She likes what our money can buy. Don't forget that when she turns the screws again.'

'Business, Leon,' Nick tersely reminded him, and he went.

On edge, disgruntled with his world, Nick turned to his computer, switched it on, and tried to settle himself to work. But Leon's words stuck in his mind. The flaming row he'd had with Tanya had ended with her saying that the party would be his last chance with her. If he hadn't made some move to reorganise his life…

His lips thinned. She'd gone too far, expecting him to order his life to suit her. It wasn't as if he was being unfaithful, taking out other women on the side.

And she certainly didn't mind him spending the big money he earned, always asking him to take her to the most fashionable restaurants and get the best seats at the live shows she wanted to see. Leon was right about her suckering him for all he could give.

Not that it was an overly disturbing factor. What was money for, anyway, if not to buy life's pleasures? Except Tanya wasn't delivering much in the way of pleasure herself. In fact, she *was* becoming an unreasonable nag, picking fights at the end of the night which inevitably turned him off wanting to have sex with her. It wasn't so much energy he lacked, but desire.

His last chance...

He had a good mind to finish it before the party, which of course she didn't want to miss. Who would? Leon had organised a marquee on Observatory Hill overlooking Sydney Harbour, a hot jazz band, top caterers. All the young successful men who were making their mark in business would be there for her to cast her eyes over.

Let her, Nick thought grimly.

Maybe he would cast his eyes around, too. There had to be someone who'd be more amenable to his needs... who wouldn't mind occupying her own shelf while he dealt with the stimulating challenge of business. He could certainly do without an unreasonable nag.

Leon headed for his own private office, hoping he'd just spiked Tanya's guns with that last comment—

selfish trouble-making bitch. She pumped Nick for all he was worth and never gave anything back, as far as Leon could see. Maybe he should rope in some hot party girls for Nick's birthday bash, show him there were many more fish in the sea, fish that would only be too happy to swim with him without kicking up a storm.

Better still....

Leon smiled.

Why not a fairy princess doll? With a magic wand that would turn Tanya Wells into an ugly croaking frog.

The smile broadened to a gleeful grin.

'Party Poppers,' Sue Olsen announced brightly, tucking the telephone receiver on her shoulder as she reached for pad and pen, hopeful of a lucrative booking. 'How may we pop for you?'

'You supply acts for birthday parties?' a male voice answered.

'Yes, indeed, sir. What do you have in mind? We have The Singing Sunflowers, The Cuddly Animal Farm, The Jellybean...'

'I want a fairy princess with a magic wand to sing "Happy Birthday" and sprinkle some sparkle around,' came the decisive demand.

Sue grinned at her friend and business partner, Barbie Lamb, who still felt ragged from yesterday's clown act for thirty screaming five-year-olds. 'We have the perfect fairy princess for you,' she answered with proud confidence.

Barbie rolled tired eyes at Sue. Clearly she needed a sprinkle of magic dust herself to raise some enthusiasm this morning. Four children's parties over the weekend was a heavy schedule and a huge energy-sucker. On the bright side, the fairy princess job would be a breeze for her, much easier to carry off than the clown act.

'What date are we looking at?' Sue inquired of the caller.

'I want to be sure of the goods first,' came the wary reply. 'Perfect, you said. I need beautiful…'

'Absolutely beautiful,' Sue assured him, grinning at Barbie.

'Long blond hair? All loose…like flowing around her shoulders?'

'That describes her hair exactly.'

'It's not a wig? A wig won't do.'

'I promise you it's not a wig.'

'Fine. What about her smile? Good teeth? A big warm smile?'

'A dazzling smile. Any dentist would be proud of her.'

'Dazzling, huh? Well, that fits the bill so far. How tall is she?'

'Tall?' Sue frowned over this requirement.

'I don't want a midget. I mean, we're not talking a dressed-up kid here, are we?'

'No. Our fairy princess is a beautiful young woman, taller than average but not quite model height.'

Barbie pulled a face, distorting her lovely features,

baring her teeth and raking out her hair to produce her Wicked Witch of the West look. Sue poked out her tongue.

'Great!' her caller enthused. 'This is sounding good. Just one more question. How does her figure rate?'

'I beg your pardon?'

'Her figure. You know...curves in the right places?'

'Uh-huh,' Sue said non-committally, waiting to see how far he would go on this contentious point.

'A skinny rake won't do,' he stated emphatically. 'If she's got sexy curves, that's the ticket.'

'Hmm...' *Sexy* set off alarm bells in Sue's mind and raised a nasty suspicion. They did occasionally get weirdo calls. Time to nail this one down. 'Is this booking for a children's party, sir?'

'No. No kids at *this* party.'

'Would this happen to be a bucks' night?' Sue asked sweetly, ready to pour acid on the idea.

'Believe me. Weddings are not in the air,' he answered sardonically. 'This is a big party for my friend's thirtieth birthday and I want this act as a special surprise for him.'

'Will there be women as well as men in attendance?'

'There most certainly will. You could say the bachelors and spinsters of the social-climbing crème of Sydney society will be there. Nothing secret or closeted about this party, I assure you,' he added, catching the wary drift of her questions. 'Very public. It's to be held in a marquee on Observatory Hill.'

'I see.' Opportunity leapt to the fore in Sue's thinking. A bunch of eligible bachelors on the loose was an attractive proposition. 'Well, I would have to insist on accompanying my fairy princess to ensure she isn't subjected to any...shall we say, indignities?'

'No problem. You're welcome to join in the party afterwards,' he offered, striking precisely the bargain Sue had been angling for. 'I take it she *does* look sexy,' he added, wanting confirmation.

Caution dictated Sue's reply. 'Her figure is definitely curvy in all the right proportions. But I wouldn't want anyone to get any wrong ideas about why she's there. This is simply a fairy princess appearance to sing "Happy Birthday." Correct?'

'Spot-on. Oh! Forgot to ask. Can she sing? I mean...*really* sing.'

'She has toured the country as a professional entertainer. Good enough?'

'Fabulous!'

This is going to cost you big, Mister, Sue decided, as she proceeded to get party details and settle on the fee, which she enterprisingly quadrupled for both herself and Barbie since it was an after-hours' engagement...plus danger money. Not that she thought there was any real danger in it but she felt such a consideration was easily justified.

Barbie was stunned at the outrageous fee Sue was demanding for this gig. No problem about making a profit next week, she thought gratefully. Ever since they'd started *Party Poppers,* they'd been battling to make ends meet, but at least it brought in more regular work than their Country and Western act, and they were settled back in Sydney. Travelling around the country-club circuit had been fun but not exactly financially rewarding.

However, listening to Sue talking on the phone, it was clear the engagement she was arranging was not about entertaining children at all. It sounded somewhat dodgy. Admittedly running a car and paying the rent on this two-bedroom apartment in Ryde, not to mention buying food and paying other bills, meant they couldn't look a gift-horse in the mouth, but...

The telephone receiver clattered down. 'Got it!' Sue cried triumphantly, dollar signs sparkling in her wickedly gleeful green eyes. She could do a great pixie or Tinkerbell with her short, ragamuffin red hair and her slim, rather petite figure, and she was definitely projecting a high degree of mischief right now.

'Got what exactly?' Barbie demanded warily.

'He didn't even hesitate over the money. Shows he's really loaded and doesn't mind spending. I just *love* men like that,' Sue bubbled on.

'Sure he's not a dirty old man?'

Sue grinned. 'Could be a dirty young man. Definitely young, thirtyish, and a bachelor. Co-owner of Multi-Media Promotions.' She cocked her head on one side. 'Maybe I could ask him to set up a website for us. Get clients from the Internet.'

'We haven't even got a computer,' Barbie dryly

reminded her. Sue's mind invariably soared with wild dreams and pulling her feet back onto the ground was often a difficult task.

She shrugged. 'Just thinking ahead. This is really good for us, Barbie. All that lovely money and opportunity plus.'

'When you get your head out of the clouds with silver lining, would you mind spelling out what this is all about?'

She did, virtually dancing around their small living room in excitement as she laid out the party details and the invitation to stay on and mix with the crème of Sydney bachelors. Which Barbie had to concede, did sound interesting, given their current dearth of social life.

'What's this guy's name? The one who booked my fairy princess act,' she asked, wondering if there was some way of checking out his *bona fides* before the night.

'Leon Webster.'

It struck a nerve and the twang was highly unpleasant. 'Leon...' Hadn't Nick Armstrong had a friend of that name, a guy full of slick patter whom he'd linked up with in his university years? Compelled to know for sure, she asked, 'And his partner's name? The birthday boy?'

'Nick Armstrong.' Sue broke into mad song. 'Happy birthday, dear Nick. Happy birthday, dear Nick....'

'Stop it!' Barbie yelled, rising from her chair with

clenched fists, so violent was the rush of emotion *that name* had stirred.

Sue stopped dead, gawking at her as though she were mad. 'What's the matter?'

As quickly as shock had drained the blood from her face, the memory of the worst hurt and humiliation of her life poured heat back into it. 'Don't you remember?'

'Remember what?' Obvious bewilderment.

Above flaming cheeks Barbie's silver-grey eyes turned to icy daggers as *she* remembered the man who'd broken her heart into irrecoverable little pieces. 'Nine years ago I sang at Nick Armstrong's twenty-first birthday party.'

Sue still looked non-plussed. 'You did?'

'Yes, I did. And I poured it all out to you at the time...how he...' She bit off the wretched recollection and faced Sue with blazing resolve. 'I will never...ever...sing for him again!'

'But...uh-oh!' The memory finally caught up with her. She grimaced. 'The guy you had the big crush on when we were schoolkids.'

'I was sixteen!' Barbie's voice shook with the violence of feeling the memory stirred.

She'd *loved* Nick Armstrong with all she was, and he'd totally belittled that love by preferring what a sexy tart with a flash car could give him. Which undoubtedly proved he wasn't the person she'd believed he was, but even telling herself he had to be a shallow rat to be seduced by such superficial assets, did not stop her from feeling utterly crushed.

'A lot of water under the bridge since then, Barbie,' Sue pleaded.

True, yet she'd carried that deep misery with her all the way. No other man had even scratched the surface of what she'd once felt for Nick Armstrong. He'd blighted her faith in love and had probably blighted her belief in dreams, too.

'It's only a ten-minute act,' Sue argued. 'It will put us well in the black financially.' Her hands lifted in appeal. 'He probably won't even recognise you. You had braces on your teeth then. Your hair was short and much fairer, almost white...'

Yes, white and crinkly like a baby lamb's coat. *Baa-Baa* Lamb was what Nick's friends had called her in those days, teasing her for following them around. She'd hated it.

'You wore glasses instead of contacts,' Sue rattled on. 'And well...you were a skinny rake when we were teenagers. You're much more mature in your looks now.'

'That's not the point,' she flared. 'I won't sing for *him*. You can if you want, Sue.'

'Oh, yeah...like I'm blond and beautiful and sexy. Come on, Barbie, the fairy princess act is yours, not mine. Besides which, I promised Leon Webster no wig.'

'Cancel then. Let him find someone else.'

'And lose all that lovely money? Not to mention the chance to rub elbows—and possibly more—with guys on the rise?' She shook her head and advanced on Barbie, the glint of determined battle in her eyes.

'Best for you to sit down, calm down, and think reasonably about this. If the thought of Nick Armstrong can hurt you so much after nine years…you've got a real problem, and it's time you faced it and got over it.'

Barbie sat down, not wanting to fight with her friend but mutinously resolved on sticking to her guns. She would not sing for Nick Armstrong. Never!

'Remember the other side of our business—*Drop Dead Deliveries?*' Sue prompted as she propped herself on the large padded armrest of the chair.

The idea of someone delivering a bunch of dead roses to a party who had injured them had appealed to quite a few clients. It was a relatively harmless outlet for feelings of frustration and anger, a *healthy* outlet, Sue had argued, when Barbie had voiced doubts. At least it stopped people doing worse and gave them the satisfaction of doing *something* instead of just being a victim. Which was probably true.

Nevertheless, Barbie preferred to pass on those jobs to Sue who liked doing them. She didn't. And delivering wilted flowers to Nick Armstrong to demonstrate what she thought of him and his actions was no answer. She wanted no contact with him at all.

'Forget it, Sue. I'd rather face a tiger snake, and you know how I feel about snakes.'

With an expressive shudder, Barbie leaned the other way, resting her elbow on the other armrest and adopting an air of unwearable-down patience. Her friend could rail at her as much as she liked, but on this issue, she would not be moved.

'Forget the dead roses. That's not what I've got in mind,' Sue assured her.

'Then why bring it up?'

'Because there's nothing like a bit of revenge when someone's done the dirty on you,' Sue went on, beginning to wax lyrical with their own advertising copy. 'Having the last laugh is wonderful. You can then get on with your life, knowing you squared the ledger. Clean slate.'

Barbie rolled exasperated eyes at her.

It didn't stop Sue.

'Revenge *is* sweet,' she declared with relish, her eyes beginning to sparkle again as she spread out her hands like a magician about to perform a marvellous illusion. 'Now imagine this, Barbie...'

CHAPTER TWO

BARBIE was literally trembling, her nerves a total jangle as she waited to make her entrance. She shouldn't have let Sue talk her into this. Somehow her friend had plumbed a well of pride, stirring it to the point where Barbie had actually thought that seeing the stunned look on Nick Armstrong's face might mend the scars on her heart. Especially when she sprinkled stardust over him, turning him into *the child*, with her being *the adult*, falsely smiling at him.

Sweet revenge, Sue called it, but right now Barbie seriously doubted that anything about this gig could turn out sweet. She would hate it if Nick Armstrong didn't recognise and remember her and she would hate it if he did. And it was useless to even try to pretend *she* had forgotten him.

Nevertheless, she was here, outside the party marquee on Observatory Hill, and it was too late to call off the promised performance. Someone inside was making a speech—Leon Webster?—to bursts of appreciative laughter and occasional guffaws. About a hundred guests, dressed in very trendy evening gear, Sue had reported, definitely a moneyed crowd.

Since the sides of the marquee were clear plastic for the guests to have an unimpeded view of the harbour and its spectacular coathanger bridge, as well as the myriad night lights of North Sydney, Barbie was standing out of sight behind their car while Sue stood at the entrance, watching proceedings until the vital moment came.

At least she could make a fast getaway, Barbie consoled herself, with the car so close by. Ten minutes—just ten minutes—of being a fairy princess and she could be out of here. Sue, of course, didn't want to leave. She was all dressed up to party in a slinky green satin slip dress—a very sexy pixie tonight—but she'd promised she would find her own way home if Barbie wanted to take off.

A burst of applause made her heart start skittering. Sue held up her hand, the signal to get ready. Barbie briefly closed her eyes and prayed that her wings wouldn't fall off, that the long train of her skirt wouldn't catch on anything, that her vocal cords wouldn't collapse on her, that the stardust mechanism on her wand would work without a hitch. One perfect performance, she pleaded, for this one night.

Leon Webster grinned around at his audience as the applause for his speech died down. 'Please…hold your seats, everyone. We have a special surprise coming up for Nick, just to add a little bit of magic to the big 3-0 milestone.'

He gestured an over-to-you to the bandleader and stepped off the podium, having stirred a buzz of speculation around the tables. Nick watched his friend striding across the dance floor to their table, a slight swagger to his gait. Leon was certainly in top form tonight. He'd pulled off a hugely entertaining speech and now he was about to pull something else out of his hat of amusing tricks.

Leon was a great party guy, Nick reflected, smiling at the high-octane energy still radiating from him as he dropped into his chair at their table. Over the years they'd had a lot of fun together—all through university, setting up the business and running it. Long-time friends and always would be, Nick thought, knowing each other probably better than any women in their lives ever would.

The band started playing something he didn't recognise until the clarinetist came in with the melody. Then Nick burst out laughing at Leon. '*"Somewhere Over the Rainbow"?*'

'The pot of gold is coming, man.'

'A bit childish, isn't it, Leon?' Tanya sniped.

Nick gritted his teeth, biting down on the urge to tell Tanya to take a hike. She'd been in a picky mood all evening—criticising everything—and very soon now he was going to advise her to join another table.

Leon gave her a smile that smacked of sweet satisfaction. 'I'm giving Nick a touch of romance, Tanya. He needs it.'

Nick felt Tanya bristle and braced himself for another snide sling off at him. The surprised exclamations of 'Oh, look!' and 'Wow!' from other guests came as welcome relief, drawing their attention to where everyone else was turning. Swivelling around in his chair, Nick was initially hit with stunned disbelief.

A gorgeous glittering blonde with gossamer wings?

Then he took in the total image and barely stifled a glorious bubble of laughter. Leon—with undoubtedly the most wickedly Machiavellian pleasure—had got him a fairy princess with a magic wand! Tanya, of course, would not appreciate the joke, but Nick no longer cared what Tanya thought. Or did. In fact, if a wave of that wand could make her disappear, he'd have no objection at all.

He smiled at the fairy princess. He wouldn't be leaving *her* on a shelf for long if he had her in his keeping, and he wouldn't need any magic to spark off desire, either. She was the best-looking fantasy he'd even seen in the flesh.

And what flesh!

The gauzy silver evening dress shimmered around hourglass curves and the clingy fabric clearly revealed there was no artful underwear involved in creating the sexy effect. This was all living, breathing *woman,* so perfect she could have emerged from the pages of a fairytale.

Her lovely face was made even more luminous by a smile that could have made gooey mush out of a stone heart and eyes that sparkled through a sprinkling of stardust. A delicate diamanté tiara crowned a long rippling flow of silky blond hair which looked all the more beautiful, framed by the wings with their fine network of silver spokes and loops.

A princess indeed, Nick thought, and hoped she would grant his wish for her to stay on at the party so they could work some magic together.

* * *

So far, so good, Barbie told herself, smiling so hard her face ached. She'd made it up the aisle between the tables from the entrance to the dance floor without a falter or mishap. Her *surprise* appearance was certainly coming off as a surprise and she was intensely grateful that the response from the guests was positive—no cat-calling or anything off-putting, just a buzz of wonder and appreciation and a heightened sense of anticipation for what would happen next.

She spotted Nick Armstrong as she stepped onto the dance floor. Leon had told Sue that he and the birthday boy would be at the table directly opposite where the band was set up, and there they both were, Leon emphatically pointing at Nick to identify him as the guest of honour.

Barbie nodded to show she understood. Nick was happily smiling at her, looking even more handsome than she remembered him, a dark blue shirt enhancing his dark colouring and heightening the vivid blue of his eyes…eyes that were gobbling her up as though she were everything his heart could desire.

For a moment, *her* heart leapt with treacherous joy… Nick loving the image of her. Then her mind savagely kicked in—*lust, not love, you fool.* He'd probably have the same look for a curvaceous bikini girl popping out of a birthday cake.

Her gaze slid briefly to the woman sitting next to him—masses of black hair in a tousled mane, pouty red lips and a red dress with a décolletage that had undoubtedly attracted him—out of the same mould as the scarlet tart he'd preferred to *true love* on his twenty-first birthday.

Barbie hated her on sight. And quite clearly, the woman was making no bones about hating her right back. The fairy princess for Nick was not going down at all well with her.

Unaccountably a sweet sense of satisfaction swept through Barbie. She bestowed an especially warm smile on Nick before turning to walk to the podium where the microphone awaited. Let him lust after her instead of his black-haired bed-pet, she thought wickedly, and put a more seductive sway into her hips to help him focus his attention where she wanted it.

Sue was right about revenge. It would be balm to her wounded soul if Nick ended up panting after her tonight. Of course, it would mean he *was* a shallow rat, but proving that beyond a doubt might help to finally put him behind her. And then she could crush him and walk away. Walk away forever!

She timed her arrival at the podium to the last chords of 'Somewhere Over the Rainbow.' The musicians were grinning at her, thoroughly enjoying the effectiveness of her appearance. The bandleader winked his approval and another wicked idea slid into her mind.

'Remember Marilyn Monroe singing "Happy Birthday" to the president?' she whispered.

He nodded, his eyes twinkling with mischief.

'I want that tempo. Okay?'

'You got it, babe.'

She took the microphone and swallowed a couple

of times to moisten her throat. One of her talents was doing a good mimic. She hoped she could pull this one off tonight. It was worth trying, anyway, she boldly reasoned, even if her voice did waver off the note. If it was sexiness that turned Nick Armstrong on, she'd pour it out at him.

The audience settled and hushed. Sue gave her a thumbs up sign from where she still stood at the entrance to the marquee. Leon Webster leaned forward, saying something to Nick at their table. The black-haired sexpot looked furious. Nick flashed a grin at his friend, ignored the woman beside him, turning his back to her as he concentrated his attention on the fairy princess about to sing for him. Not polite attention, Barbie noted triumphantly. Wolfish attention!

The band struck up a vibrant opening chord. Barbie took a deep breath and lifted the microphone close to her mouth so she could purr into it.

'Ha...ppy birth...day...' another big breath '...dear... Nick...'

A ripple of amusement ran around the marquee. It was pure over-the-top candied honey. Nick tilted his head back in delight, a low chuckle emerging from his throat...music to Barbie's ears. He was captivated all right.

She repeated the line, putting a huskier edge on her voice. The band paused for her until the appreciative laughter died down, picking up again as she started the third 'Happy Birthday', soaring with her as she poured more volume into the high note, then dropping softly to the 'Dear Ni…ick,' into which she pumped a load of seductive come-on.

He was not the least bit embarrassed by it. His head was cocked slightly to one side, as though bewitched and bemused, wanting more.

Barbie gave it to him, drawing out the last line and loading it with sensual innuendo as she sang '…to…you-ou-ou,' her lips rounded in a suggestive oval, sending a long, long, visual kiss.

The crowd in the marquee erupted then, guys standing up on chairs, clapping and hooting and whistling, the women laughing and cheering. Leon Webster jumped to his feet, arms up in the air, drinking in the credit of being a magnificent impresario to have brought this off.

But Nick didn't even glance at his friend. Or at his rollicking guests. His gaze was burning up a line that linked him straight to his fairy princess, and Barbie didn't feel her face ache at all as she smiled some sizzling heat right back at him. She replaced the microphone on its stand and stepped down from the podium, all primed for the final part of her act.

'Everybody join in singing now,' Leon shouted, swinging around and waving up more enthusiasm.

The band broke into a more jolly rendition of 'Happy Birthday' and everyone who wasn't already standing, rose to give loud voice in accolade to the one man who remained seated. Hands slid over his shoulders as Barbie walked towards him, her wand benevolently raised—hands with long red nails, claiming jealous possession.

If Nick felt them he showed no sign of it. No appeasing smile was flashed at the woman behind him. His gaze remained fixed on the princess approaching him, feasting on every physical facet of the illusion.

Barbie feasted on the sense of power this gave her. It was more exhilarating than any applause she had ever received for entertaining people. This was real woman-power and she was holding it over the one man in the world she most wanted to hold it over... Nick Armstrong.

Her stomach was contracting in spasms of delight. Her breasts seemed to thrust themselves out more, peaking and tingling. Her hips rolled in voluptuous provocation, her thighs sliding sensuously against each other with every step she took towards him. She was intensely conscious of every part of her femininity, as though it had not only been awakened to a new level of awareness, but aroused to fever-pitch and highly primitive immediacy.

Nick was facing her, still seated, but with his face upturned when she stopped in front of him, barely a step away. It was a miracle she remembered what had to be done with the wand. His eyes were locked on hers, transmitting a blazing quest for more knowledge of her, intimate knowledge of her, and the desire to get it.

'Make a wish,' she invited huskily, smiling as she lifted the wand over his head and pressed the button on the silver rod, opening the star at the end of it to release a shower of silver glitter. It speckled his hair, his nose, his cheeks, and the brilliant blue of his eyes suddenly seemed to become more piercing, magnetic in its intensity.

She bent to bestow a fairy kiss on his cheek. Her heart was drumming in her ears, driving the noise around them off to some far distance. She saw his lips part slightly and temptation seized her. Instead of planting her mouth where it should have been planted to seal the wish-spell, an irresistible force dragged it down to meet his.

The moment the first tantalising contact was made was the last Barbie had any control over. Nick surged to his feet, a thumb hooked under her chin, fingers thrusting into her hair, taking a firm grip, tilting her head back, his mouth dominating hers as his other arm burrowed under her wings and scooped her in to a full body blast of his highly energised masculinity.

It was like no other kiss Barbie had experienced in her whole life—a wild, storming kiss that electrified every nerve, a stampeding kiss that reduced her mind to a whirlpool of fantastic sensation, an ecstatically passionate kiss that taught her that lust had an intoxicating excitement that could not be denied. Enthralled by these overwhelming factors, she was unaware of the removal of the wand from her grasp. Indeed, she didn't even realise where her hands were.

With shocking abruptness, the mouth that had wrought such intense rapture was wrenched from hers. The harsh words, 'What the hell!' rang in her ears. Her eyes flew open just as the star at the end of her wand was slammed down on Nick's head as though it were a flyswatter being wielded with deadly intent. Glitter sprayed from the impact.

'I'll give you magic!' a woman's voice screeched, and the wand lifted, ready to crash down again.

Nick's hand hastily disengaged itself from Barbie's hair and he threw up an arm to ward off its descent. 'Quit it, Tanya!' he grated.

'*You* quit it!' came the fierce retort.

Tanya, the black-haired witch! Dazedly, Barbie stared at the furious attacker, feeling oddly detached from the emotional violence playing across the other woman's face.

'How dare you kiss *her*, in front of *me!*' she snarled as Nick swivelled to grab the damaging wand from her.

Tanya whipped it out of his reach and advanced on Barbie who was now hugged to Nick's side but open to frontal assault. The red mouth was stretched into an ugly jeer as her arm swung back to deliver another forcible blow, this time aimed at Barbie's head.

'And you...you fairy cow...can milk someone else for sex! Nick is mine!'

It was Leon Webster who caught the wand in mid-swing, tore it out of her grasp and tossed it onto the dance floor. 'Cool it, Tanya!' he commanded.

Being de-weaponed, however, did nothing to lower the raging fury. With arms raised and fingers curled like talons, Tanya lunged at Barbie, hissing like a snake.

Nick threw in a shoulder-block. Leon knocked her arms down and pinned them to her sides in a smothering hug from behind. Everything had moved so fast, Barbie was still in a shocked daze, though her body was quivering in reaction to the chaos without and within.

'Let me go!' Tanya seethed.

'Not until you're ready to behave,' Leon tersely retorted.

'Right!' another voice cracked into the maelstrom. Sue!

'No indignities you said, Mr. Webster!' she reminded him in high dudgeon. Her hands were planted on her hips in aggressive mode as she subjected Nick and Leon—still holding the struggling Tanya—to a look of arch scorn. 'The crème of young Sydney society?' she drawled with biting acid.

'Miss Olsen…Sue…' Leon started ingratiatingly.

'My fairy princess gets grabbed and ravished in plain view of a hundred people…'

'I didn't anticipate she'd be so…'

Sue cut him off. 'We delivered precisely what you ordered, sir. Sexy, you said. Indeed, you insisted.'

'I know. I know. But…'

'Control, Mr. Webster, was in your court.'

'I'm doing it. I saved her from being attacked. Tanya, apologise to the ladies.'

'Ladies! They're no better than whores!' she shrieked.

'More indignities,' Sue hammered. She glared at Nick. 'Kindly unhand my fairy princess, sir. I am taking her out of this unsavoury scene.'

His warm, supporting arm was removed, leaving

Barbie feeling chilled and shivery. He gestured a plea to Sue. 'I'm sorry things got out of hand...'

'Perhaps you'll now take them *in* hand,' Sue shot at him, glancing meaningly at Tanya. 'I expect Mr. Webster to escort us out of this marquee, guaranteeing safety for my fairy princess. And may I say, sir...' Her green eyes knifed into Nick's. '...your choice of companion is no lady.'

'Who the hell do you think you are!' Tanya snarled.

Sue ignored her, nodding to Barbie. 'The wand needs collecting.'

Barbie took a deep breath, gathering herself together, then stepped away from Nick, trying to maintain an air of dignity as she set off to where the wand had fallen on the dance floor.

'No, wait!' A hoarse plea from Nick.

Barbie hesitated, still feeling the magnetic pull he'd held on her, but she resisted it, realising Sue was right in her judgement to get them out of here, pronto! Nothing good could eventuate from what had already gone on. Revenge, she decided, was a very tricky thing to play with.

'Please...stay!'

It was an almost anguished cry from Nick this time, curling around Barbie's heart, squeezing it, throwing her into confusion. Before she could respond either way, her wings were grabbed from behind and jerked from the boned slot in the back of her dress. Crying out in horror at the damage that might be done, she swung around to find Nick juggling the wings with an equal expression of horror, babbling apologies. 'I didn't mean... I just wanted...'

'More indignities!' Sue accused hotly. 'Mr. Webster...'

'For God's sake, Nick!' Leon begged. 'Leave her be and take Tanya from me.'

'I don't *want* Tanya!' Nick snapped at him. 'She can go take a flying leap off the Harbour Bridge for all I care!'

'You scum!'

The black-haired witch broke free of Leon and smashed Barbie's wings out of Nick's hands with her fists. They fell to the floor and she jumped on them, stamping her feet all over them like a dervish, her red toenails splayed openly in black stilleto sandals, looking like drops of blood on the silvery gossamer as she wreaked her malicious damage.

Sheer shock paralysed everyone for several seconds.

'No...no...' Barbie moaned.

It shot Nick into action, hauling the hysterical woman off her feet and carrying her to the other side of the table where he forcibly held her to prevent any more harm being done.

Barbie stared down at the broken wings. They'd taken her so many hours to create and they'd been beautiful. Tears welled into her eyes. It was like a desecration...

Someone tapped her on the arm and offered her the wand she'd meant to collect. The star was hanging drunkenly at the end of the silver rod. It was broken, too.

'You're going to get a huge damage bill for this, Mr. Webster,' Sue threatened darkly, folding her arms in firm belligerent style.

'Okay. I'll pay,' he promised on a ragged sigh. 'If we could move now…'

They moved, Leon shepherding both Sue and Barbie through the loud melee in the marquee. The wings were left where they lay crushed. Leon muttered something about a good joke going awry. Sue castigated him for not providing adequate protection. Barbie stared at the battered wand in her hand.

A falling star, she thought.

A wish…

Did wishes ever come true?

CHAPTER THREE

LEON swept into Nick's office for their usual Monday morning conference, hoping his friend had wiped the birthday disaster from their joint slate, only to be faced with incontrovertible evidence that Nick was still obsessed with it!

'What are those fairy wings doing on your desk?' he demanded in exasperation.

Nick lifted a belligerently determined face. 'I'm going to fix them.'

'And just how do you propose to do that? Tanya punched so many holes through them with her stiletto heels, the fabric is irreparable.'

'I am aware of that, Leon.' He glowered dangerously. 'Which is why I need to get the fabric matched so I can replace it. I decided you wouldn't mind lending me your secretary for a while this morning. She'd probably know how...'

'You can't use Sharon for personal jobs.'

One black eyebrow lifted in challenge. 'Can't I?'

'This is ridiculous!' Leon expostulated. 'I said I'd pay the bill for damages and I will. As soon as it comes in.'

'I'm going to fix the wings,' Nick repeated stubbornly.

'Why?'

'Because I want to. Because it will mean something when I give them back to her.'

Leon expelled a long breath. Nick was definitely out of his tree. He lifted his hands in a plea for sanity. 'It was just an act. An act I paid for, Nick. Nothing more. Just a...'

'It turned into something more.'

'Okay, she was beautiful. She was sexy. She turned you on. But you don't even know the woman, Nick. She might be...'

'I don't care who she is!' His hand slammed down on the desk as he stood up. 'I want to feel that again. I have to know. And I *will* know.' He paced around the office, clearly disturbed, his hands moving in agitated gestures. 'When I kissed her... I've never experienced anything like it in my life before. She's different, Leon.'

'Fairy princesses tend to be different, Nick. Kind of like dream stuff.'

That perfectly rational point earned a flash of impatience that said he didn't understand, didn't have the experience to understand.

'I can't let it go,' came the steely resolve.

Totally out of his tree!

Recognising a brick wall when he saw it, Leon asked, 'So, have you tracked her down, arranged to meet under normal circumstances?'

Nick's face twisted with frustration. 'I called and called the *Party Poppers* number yesterday and all I got was an answering machine. Then finally, this morning, I reached that Sue Olsen on the phone, but she flatly refused to give out the name and address of her fairy princess. Against company policy.'

Dead right, Leon thought approvingly. Fantasy and reality didn't mix. Expectations could never be met and it was a stupid waste of time to go chasing them.

Nick grimaced and muttered, 'But I'll get it somehow. Sue Olsen said something about *Singing Sunflowers* before I started in on questions. I'll ask my sister to book that act for her kids. My fairy princess is a singer...right? She might be a sunflower, too.'

The desperate hope in Nick's voice told Leon his friend needed help fast or very little creative work was going to get done on the designs they'd been contracted to deliver. He instantly revised his opinion. The sooner hopes and expectations were blasted, the better.

'No need to go to that trouble, Nick,' he soothed.

'I'll go to any lengths,' came the punchy retort, his eyes flashing unshakable determination. 'I have to find her.'

'Sure you do. I understand,' Leon quickly inserted. 'All I meant was...leave it to me. I'll have the name and address you want before today is out.'

Nick frowned, suspicious of his confidence. 'How?' he demanded.

'I'll call Sue Olsen, ask her out for lunch as an apology for the mess on Saturday night. Restaurant of her choice. Promise to write out a cheque for the damages bill there and then. Butter her up. Piece of cake. As you well know, I am the best salesman in the business.'

'What about her company policy?'

'I'll find a loophole. Trust me.'

Nick expelled a deep sigh. Then his eyes narrowed. 'You won't put her further offside?'

Leon laughed. 'That feisty little redhead wasn't offside. She was making hay while the sun shone. A dyed-in-the-wool opportunist, like me. In fact, I'll enjoy having lunch with her. I have the feeling Miss Olsen and I speak the same language.'

'Okay. Just don't slip up, Leon. This is really important to me.'

'No problem, Nick, I swear. Just shovel those wings off your desk and get to work while I…'

'I'm still going to fix them. If you'd send Sharon along…'

Leon ungritted his teeth enough to bite out, 'Okay. But don't take up too much office time on it. It's bad business getting secretaries to do personal jobs, Nick, and you've got a full schedule, too.'

'I just want to ask her advice,' he insisted.

'Fine! Speak to you later.'

Leon went off fuming.

Women!

He'd got rid of Tanya Wells for good, only to be loaded with another festering problem. There was black irony for you. A fairy princess was supposed to remove trouble not make it. He should have hired a doll, not a real woman. Big mistake, Leon, he castigated himself. Though there was one bright spot.

A very feisty little redhead.

Cute, too.

He wouldn't mind having lunch with Sue Olsen at all.

Yes, that was definitely a bright spot.

Barbie was still trying to mend the broken wand when the *Drop Dead Deliveries* telephone rang. She frowned at it. Sue had gone off to lunch with Leon Webster, assured of getting the damages cheque, while she was supposed to deal personally with any bookings that came in. Except Barbie didn't like answering the *revenge* phone, as she thought of it. Why couldn't it have been the *Party Poppers* one?

'Business is business,' she muttered, putting the wand down with a resigned sigh.

Feeling very, very ambivalent about revenge after the cataclysmic meeting with Nick Armstrong, she reluctantly lifted the receiver and pulled an order pad and pen within easy reach.

'*Drop Dead Deliveries,*' she stated flatly, unable to project Sue's enthusiasm. 'How may I help you?'

'I want you to deliver a dozen dead roses to a guy named Nick Armstrong at *Multi-Media Promotions.*'

Barbie's heart flipped.

Was this the black-haired witch who had attacked them with the wand and smashed her wings?

'Your name please?' she asked.

'Tanya Wells.'

Tanya! No mistake about that. Even the voice was

putting her teeth on edge—like chalk screeching on a blackboard.

'And I want you to write just one word on the card—*Loser!*'

'You don't want to add your name?'

'He'll know who it's from,' came the venomous retort. 'And before we go any further I want to know when you can deliver. It has to be today and the sooner the better.'

The demanding tone raised Barbie's hackles. This was definitely a woman who wanted—and expected—to get everything her own way. Nevertheless, a paying customer was entitled to the service they paid for.

'Just a moment while I check,' she said with surface calm, hiding the maelstrom of thoughts the other woman stirred.

Loser! Well, *she* had tickets on herself that Barbie would never have given her, but maybe Tanya Wells had reason to believe Nick valued his relationship with her. If he did, he'd certainly been a fool to act as he had at his birthday party. On the other hand, maybe all women had only one value for him, and he thought he'd found another candidate to fulfil that requirement better than Tanya. Was that why he was so hot for Barbie's name and address?

'Well? When can you get the dead roses to him?' Angry impatience.

'Possibly three o'clock,' Barbie temporised, feeling distinctly negative about obliging Tanya Wells with anything.

'Can't you do it earlier?'

Not if Sue did the job. But what if she went herself? Dressed in a black suit with her hair tucked up under a hat, dark glasses on...the image she'd present would be a far cry from the fairy princess that had taken Nick's fancy on Saturday night. And if he did somehow recognise her, she could deliver a double whammy of rejection. Serve him right for playing fast and loose!

At least he hadn't identified her as Barbie Lamb, so she felt safe about that. No humiliating trip down memory lane would eventuate from this. And it would be...interesting...just to see him again, in his workplace.

Temptation was a terrible, terrible thing.

'We could manage two o'clock if that suits.' It was almost twelve now. She needed time to get dressed...

'Perfect! That should screw up his precious work this afternoon.'

Again Barbie frowned. Tanya Wells was a malicious piece of goods and it didn't sit well, being a partner to her wishes. Yet how could she judge what had actually gone on between her and Nick? Maybe she had just cause...if he *was* a shallow rat!

'May I have your credit card details, Miss Wells?'

Barbie completed the transaction, her mind moving into a ferment over the wisdom of taking this job. Nick's calls to *Party Poppers* proved he wanted to see her again, but he didn't know who she was and Barbie found herself totally churned up over what his response would be if he found out. A sexy fantasy was one thing, reality quite another.

She'd certainly found out what it was like to be kissed by him—with lustful desire. And she couldn't deny she'd felt swamped by lustful desire herself. But undoubtedly it had been no more than a highly heated moment, generated by volatile emotions on both sides. His angry outburst about not caring if Tanya took a flying leap off the Harbour Bridge surely pointed to their having been at odds before Barbie had appeared on the scene as a fairy princess.

Revenge...

For all she knew, Nick himself might have been taking vengeance on Tanya for something the black-haired witch had done!

Barbie stared at the order sheet she had just written out.

Maybe she shouldn't go.

Sue could do it when she came back from her lunch with Leon Webster. So what if the delivery was a bit late...

No!

She wanted to see Nick for herself, *in the cold light of day!* Sue was right about finishing this...this hangover from the past. Saturday night was supposed to have achieved that purpose, yet when he'd kissed her...somehow it had just made everything worse, stirring up what she had wanted to put behind her. It would be different today.

Best to go and make absolutely certain there was nothing about Nick Armstrong that was worth harbouring in her memory.

CHAPTER FOUR

NICK propped the broken wings as best he could against the file cabinet, then moved a chair up beside them. The small swatch of damaged fabric he'd cut out of one of them made them look even more forlorn, but the salesman at the Strand Arcade where Sharon had advised him to go, swore the organza he'd subsequently bought was a perfect match. Not feeling quite so certain, Nick wanted to check it truly was right.

He undid the parcel, shook out the full length of the folded organza and draped it over the chair next to the wings. Moving back a few paces, he looked from one to the other and felt both relief and satisfaction. The salesman did know his fabrics. It *was* exactly the same.

A rather tentative knock on his office door brought a smile to his face. It was sure to be Sharon coming to see if he'd been successful in his lunch-hour quest. 'Come in,' he called, not even glancing at the door, his smiling gaze revelling in the evidence of his achievement.

Barbie took a deep breath. It had been bad enough running the gauntlet of curious stares on her way to this door. The receptionist had looked very doubtful about giving directions to Nick Armstrong's office, and Barbie had been fearful of being called back and more rigorously questioned. But she'd made it to here without being accosted—the all-black funereal garb probably an intimidating factor that had worked for her—and now she was being invited to enter by *his* voice.

She had to go through with it.

Stupid not to, at this point.

Nevertheless, her heart was thumping erratically as she turned the knob and pushed the door open. Her mind was so highly energised, she had the weird sensation of floating as her quivering legs took the few necessary steps to move into the room to face the man and the feelings she'd come to confront.

Except he wasn't facing her at all.

Nor even looking at her.

His attention was trained entirely on...*her fairy princess wings!*

'See?' he said, gesturing to a length of fabric draped over a nearby chair. 'A perfect match!'

Shock held Barbie speechless. Her gaze moved slowly from the silvery organza to the man who had gone to the trouble of acquiring it. Would a shallow rat want to fix her wings? Wasn't Leon Webster in the process of paying the cost of replacing them? What was going on here?

She wished she could read Nick's mind. His expression in profile seemed relaxed into a smile, but what did the smile mean? Was he remembering her as the fairy princess, anticipating more from her? Or calculating how to get more?

A convulsive little shiver ran down her spine as she stared at him. He was so very handsome, even in profile, so strongly male. His thick black hair brushed the collar of his white shirt. He had the broad shoulders of a star swimmer and a taut sexy butt, outlined by the grey trousers he wore. She remembered her thighs being pressed to the hard ungiving muscularity of his, her breasts squashing against the hot wall of his chest...

Her nerves leapt in shock as he suddenly turned, looking directly at her, his vivid blue eyes sharp and probing. The lingering smile was instantly wiped from his face and a frown creased his brow as his gaze raked her from head to foot and back again.

Panic plunged Barbie's mind into a fog of fear and set her heart fluttering in wild agitation. Would he—could he—recognise her, despite the large dark sunglasses and the black hat that covered her hair and dipped over her forehead? Her fingers closed more tightly around the base of the cone of black tissue paper which held the dead roses. She could use it as a self-protective weapon if she had to.

'Who *are* you?' he rapped out.

Relief! He didn't know. Barbie struggled to regather her wits. She was here to do a job, not get shattered again by this man. Every self-protective instinct screamed—*get it right and go.*

'Mr. Nick Armstrong?'

Her voice came out too soft and husky. She should

have swallowed first. He was frowning more quizzically at her now. Had her tone struck a familiar chord with him? Was he matching it to the way she'd sung at his birthday party?

'Yes,' he answered belatedly, his gaze zeroing in on her mouth, studying it with highly discomforting intensity.

Barbie was drawn into staring back at his, remembering how it had felt, how it had aroused such a stampede of wild sensations and needs...

Rattled at finding herself so treacherously distracted from her purpose, she rushed into the set speech for this job. 'I hereby present you with a *Drop Dead Delivery*.'

'What?' he demanded incredulously.

Her nerves jangled at the sharpness of his tone. Somehow she found the strength of will to step forward, holding out the bundle of black tissue for him to take. 'This was ordered for you,' she explained.

'By whom?'

He didn't take delivery. His arms remained at his sides, his refusal to accept her offering an innate challenge to her presence, and by stepping closer to him, Barbie had the overwhelming sense of having put herself in a danger zone. It was as though he emitted an electric charge. Her whole body was tingling with an extreme awareness of his powerful masculinity. She wished she could turn tail and run but knew instinctively he wouldn't let her.

The black tissue paper rustled slightly. She was shaking. Desperate to get past this contretemps with him, she quickly spelled out, 'I understand from our client that you will know who the sender is.'

'Someone who wants me to *drop dead?*' he quizzed sardonically, still not taking delivery. His eyes were like blue lasers, boring through the dark cover of her sunglasses. 'Now who would that be?'

The lenses were impenetrable, weren't they? He couldn't possibly see through them. Barbie took a deep breath to quell the frantic fears and his gaze instantly dropped to the heave of her chest, obviously noting the strain of her full breasts against her figure-hugging suitcoat.

'I am merely the messenger, sir,' she gabbled, appalled by the responsive hardening of her nipples.

His gaze slowly trailed up her long throat, paused at her mouth again, then lifted to her sunglasses. 'I see,' he drawled.

What did he see?

If he did recognise her, what did she want to do about it? What did she really want? How could Nick Armstrong spark so much...*response* in her? This wasn't a hangover from the past. This was here and now!

'A messenger, dressed in mourning,' he continued. 'No doubt emphasising that the gift is a very black mark against me. And you are paid to perform this act. To the hilt, one might say.'

Feeling like a pinned butterfly, Barbie squirmed inwardly at his summing up. 'Yes, I'm paid to do it,' she acknowledged.

His face hardened and there was a mocking glint

in his eyes as he said, 'You obviously take pride in superb attention to detail. Do you carry through all your paid performances...to the hilt?'

He knew.

Barbie could feel it in her bones.

And he didn't like it. He didn't like it one bit.

While she felt trapped in a cage of her own making, he reached out and snatched the cone of black tissue from her, leaving her unshielded from his gaze which once again raked her from head to toe, not so much inspecting the black funereal attire this time but very definitely taking in the shapeliness of her figure, making her burn with the sense he was matching it up in his mind to the memory of another act.

Why did she feel so guilty? She hadn't done anything wrong, had she? This whole thing had started as a need to put a painful memory to rest, simply a means to a justifiable end.

Inexorably, her gaze was drawn to the broken fairy wings, propped against a file cabinet, and the length of organza obviously bought to mend them.

Why?

What was their significance to him?

'A bunch of dead roses,' he drawled. 'Symbolic of the end of love?'

She jerked her gaze back to his and uttered the one word that had driven her here. 'Closure.' Except there could be no closure while such tantalising questions remained unanswered.

'I beg your pardon?'

'*Drop Dead Deliveries* are about closure,' she elaborated, knowing she should go. He'd taken delivery so her job was done. Yet she felt paralysed by her inner confusion.

'Ah!'

He flicked open the card and read what was written inside. *'Loser!'* His mouth curled in irony. 'Typical of Tanya, wanting to get in the last word, wanting to crawl into my mind again.' Again his expressive blue eyes mocked her purpose here. 'As it happens, she's wasted her money on this last little malicious act. It doesn't touch me. At all.'

But the fairy wings did.

They had to or they wouldn't be here.

'Do you get many clients who want this kind of closure?' he asked curiously.

'Quite a few,' she replied, deeply disquieted by his description of 'a last malicious act.' Revenge was supposed to be about balancing justice. An eye for an eye, a hurt for a hurt...

'Can the clients specify *who* does the delivery?'

It leapt into her mind that he thought Tanya had specifically asked for her to bring the dead roses to him and that she was a co-conspirator in malice. Which she was in a way, but she hadn't meant him to recognise her, to put it together...if he had.

Though she had thought of delivering a double whammy. But that was to be a payback for his playing fast and loose, and how could she link playing fast and loose to the time and trouble of buying the organza to fix her wings? Everything about this scene was wrong and Barbie had the sinking feeling there was no way to put it right.

Best to get out of here.

Fast.

'No, the messenger is simply the messenger to both parties. Anonymous,' she replied emphatically, and took a step backwards, testing her legs were steady enough for a quick escape.

'Anonymous,' he repeated, his eyes glittering in a way that shot danger signals through Barbie's entire nervous system.

'Yes,' she answered, barely able to draw breath. 'And since the delivery has now been made, please excuse me.'

She swung on her heel, heading for the open doorway, desperately needing space to rethink this whole situation with Nick Armstrong.

A hand clamped on her shoulder, forcibly halting her flight.

Then to her utter horror, her hat was yanked from her head and she felt her hair spilling from the pins she'd used to fasten it out of sight—hair that Nick was absolutely certain to connect with the fairy princess!

CHAPTER FIVE

SHEER desperation drove Barbie's reaction. It felt as though everything was zooming out of control and she had to hang on to it somehow. Her hands flew up to grab her tumbling hair and she spun around, tearing her shoulder out of Nick's grasp.

'My hat!' she shrieked at him in outraged protest.

His face was set in aggressive determination, his blue eyes blazing a mocking triumph, and he took absolutely no notice of her protest. In a lightning-fast move, he reached out and whipped off her sunglasses, leaving her face totally naked to his view. Naked and hopelessly vulnerable to positive identification. Which he made, beyond any shadow of a doubt.

'So!' His mouth curved into a nerve-shaking smile of sardonic satisfaction. 'We meet again. Quite intriguing…reincarnation.'

Barbie's mind boggled over his meaning. The shock of being so abruptly and effectively unveiled was still pounding through her. Her hands remained stuck in her hair, though any rescue operation there was now futile. All she could do was stare helplessly at him as he folded her sunglasses and tucked them into his shirt pocket.

'They're mine,' she said, fighting to regain some iota of control.

51

'Safe-keeping,' he assured her and in another star-tling action, strode right past Barbie, straight for the door which he not only closed but stood against, blocking any path to freedom. 'Safe from interruption, as well,' he declared, emanating resolute purpose.

Like a powerful magnet he'd drawn her gaze after him, and she stood half-turned, watching him, totally mesmerised by what he intended to do next. Her heart was hammering in her ears. Slowly, without any real decision-making at all, her hands slid from her hair and her arms dropped limply to her sides, defeated in their quest to ward off a moment that had come, re-gardless of her efforts to stop it. Her hat was forgot-ten. Nick Armstrong dominated her entire conscious-ness.

'From heavenly fairy princess bestowing fa-vours…to dark lady of vengeance in one fell swoop,' he commented with a wry twist of his mouth. 'Do you enjoy playing mind games?'

The shock question jolted her mind back into some semblance of working order. 'You weren't supposed to recognise me.'

His eyebrows lifted challengingly. 'So you wanted the upper hand of checking me out while I was under fire from the dearly departed Tanya.'

'Something like that,' she admitted.

'The relationship with Tanya was in its death throes before the party. Neither of us was happy with the other.'

'Then why were you still together?'

'The party was planned some time ago. It

seemed...' He shrugged. '...ungracious to retract the invitation.' His eyes glittered with a surge of desire that encompassed Barbie, stirring a host of ungovernable responses. 'Though I've regretted that mistake ever since,' he softly drawled, raising goose bumps on her skin.

'You didn't care about her feelings,' Barbie shot at him in wild defence, dredging up the nine-year-old memory of how he hadn't cared about her feelings, either. He'd thanked her for the twenty-first birthday gift she had thriftily saved to buy him, then put it aside. But when the sexy tart with the sports car gave him the same gift—albeit worth a lot more money—he'd worn it for everyone to see whose offering he prized more.

'Some feelings can override all others,' he answered.

Yes, like feelings below the belt. Nothing to do with his heart, Barbie thought, fighting to retain some sensible perspective on her experience of his actions.

'They can even reach past a superficial disguise,' he went on, stepping away from the door, towards her, instantly raising her tension and enveloping her in his as he continued talking to her. 'There I was, looking at the broken wings, and suddenly I *felt* your presence in this office.'

He couldn't, Barbie fiercely reasoned, not wanting to believe it. Probably a desire to transfer a lingering fantasy into substance.

'My scalp actually started tingling,' he said, closing the distance between them at a slow deliberate stroll.

Barbie felt her own scalp starting to tingle with the intensity of feeling he was projecting at her. Had she done that to him while she'd stood looking at him, recalling how it had felt when he'd kissed her?

'An extraordinary sensation,' he continued. 'Like a shower of magic setting off waves of intense awareness.'

Her stomach contracted, whether in panicky fear or some treacherous excitement she had no idea, but she was certainly experiencing intense awareness now as he came closer and closer. It didn't occur to her to move backwards. Her whole concentration was wrapped up in watching him. She even forgot to breathe when he gestured at her clothes.

'When I swung around to find seemingly a stranger in black, I thought all my instincts were out of kilter.' He stopped barely an arm's length away and his eyes mocked her belief in being unrecognisable. 'Then you spoke…and the voice was unmistakable.'

Her breath whooshed out on a gust of outrage. If that was true, how come he hadn't recognised it as Barbie Lamb's voice when she'd sung on Saturday night? Hadn't he even bothered to *listen* to her all those years that her family had mixed with his? Or maybe he had a short—a very short—memory span. Either way, Barbie seethed over his *recognition.*

'Angry that your deception didn't come off?'

'I don't believe you. Why remove my hat if you were so sure?'

'To stop you from leaving.'

'And my sunglasses.'

'I hate talking to people who hide their thoughts behind dark glasses. I wanted to see your eyes.'

'You had no right.'

'You walked in here to get at me. You weren't asked to do this job. You chose it, because it involved me. I think that gives me the right to ask why...and see the answer in your eyes.'

Barbie didn't want to answer him.

'You couldn't keep away?' he asked softly, seductively.

'Yes, I could,' she retorted, resenting his power to attract, even against her will. 'This was business. Why should I knock back a job because you're at the end of it? You have no power over my life, Nick Armstrong.'

His eyes flashed a sharp challenge. 'Then it won't matter if you give me your name.'

'I've given you what I've been paid to give you. You have no right to more,' she argued.

'You weren't paid to respond to my kiss as you did,' he shot at her with blazing conviction. 'And yes, Tanya did muddy the situation. But don't tell me it was only business that brought you here today. You thought it was a safe way to see...to know...if what you'd felt then could be felt again.'

Her heart felt as though it was being squeezed. She did want him—had always wanted him—but how could she feel this turbulent desire for a man who'd been so crassly insensitive to her young love? Her gaze flicked to the broken fairy wings.

'I wanted to fix them for you,' he murmured.

More easily fixed than a broken heart, she thought savagely, returning her gaze to his, her inner agitation increasing at the raw flare of need and want she saw. Did *he* have a heart to break?

'Why?' she choked out.

'Because they were part of the magic that happened between us. It was perfect, and to have anything belonging to you, or that moment of coming together, reduced to tatters, feels wrong.'

He certainly hadn't felt that way nine years ago, Barbie told herself, but somehow the reminder was losing its power to armour her against the feelings he stirred. It was different now. He cared. Or was it her own need to believe he did, pressing that view?

He reached out and gently stroked her cheek. 'It was real…what we felt. It's real now, too. Which proves it wasn't fantasy.'

Her skin heated and tingled under his touch. For the life of her she couldn't move. With feather-light fingertips he seemed to be infiltrating her bloodstream, making her pulse beat faster and faster. His voice was drumming through her brain and heart, setting off echoes she couldn't stop.

'And it wasn't one-sided. You kissed me right back. You were *with* me.'

With him…with him…with him…

The yearning welled up in her like an unstoppable tidal wave. The sexy tart with the sports car was sucked away. So was the black-haired witch, Tanya. This was *her* time with Nick…the man she'd loved, hated, dreamed about. Why not have it? Why not?

His fingers drifted into her hair. His head bent, his mouth coming closer and closer to hers. Anticipation zinged through her, blowing all worrisome thoughts away. Her whole body craved the kiss that was coming, everything within her poised to match it with that one previous, sensational experience. Would it be the same? Would it be more?

His lips brushed hers. She closed her eyes, her entire being focused on the soft sensuality of this initial pressure, an intensely erotic caress, lips sliding over hers, changing direction, exploring, tasting, his tongue delicately probing, exciting a compulsion to take some initiative herself, to gather sensory impressions of him and arouse the same excitement she felt. She didn't want it to be like a one-sided dream.

Her tentative assault on his mouth triggered a more aggressive possession of her own and Barbie was instantly caught up in a passionate entanglement that was certainly not the fluffy stuff of dreams. The wild explosion of sensation was like a cascade of fireworks, fountains of brilliant pleasure shooting in every direction, intense bursts of excitement flaring, lingering, overtaken by more and more fantastic effects.

She loved it, revelled in it, exulted in it. Her arms curled around his neck, wanting to hold him close, wanting to feel all of him as she had before Tanya had broken the spell on Saturday night, real flesh-and-blood Nick, hot and hard and male, pressing the unmistakable strength of his desire for her, man and woman surging towards an intimacy that demanded urgent fulfilment, and everything within her craving it, sizzling with need.

'Nick!'

The call of his name was like a whip-crack, slicing through their mounting enthralment, a sharp discordant intrusion on an intensely private togetherness, yet they were so deeply immersed in each other, disengagement was reluctant on both sides.

'Nick! Have you totally lost it?' came the harsh, exasperated demand.

Nick's slowly expelled breath tingled over her sensitised lips as he interrupted their kiss to growl, 'Get out, Leon.'

'Oh, great!' A jeer of fuming frustration. 'I bring Sue Olsen along to check you out personally, and the fairy princess is already history.'

Sue? Barbie's eyes flew open. Her sluggish brain snapped to red alert. Sue could mess up everything!

'I don't need help,' Nick tersely asserted, loosening his embrace, sliding one arm away from her as he half turned to put Barbie in clearer view of his friend. 'I've got her right here with me. So take yourself off, Leon.'

'Barbie!'

Shock horror from Sue, her mouth gaping as she released the fatal name that could link to a memory Barbie couldn't bear to have raised in Nick Armstrong's mind. Barbie Lamb...the horrible childhood nickname, Baa-Baa...it would ruin what they shared now. Totally ruin it. He'd start thinking about her differently, be amused instead of stirred, and he'd remember how she'd felt for him at sixteen...

Panic welled up in Barbie as she stared at her friend who was standing just to the side of Leon Webster and close to the door he'd opened, undoubtedly expecting his partner to be at work. How could she stop any further revelation?

'It *is* her!' Leon agreed in surprise, taking in the tumbling mass of blond hair on top of the very different clothing. 'In black drag?'

'A *Drop Dead Delivery* came in from the harpy who broke my fairy wings,' Barbie shot at Sue, hoping to shut her up. 'I had to come...'

'Business.' Sue caught on, collecting herself enough to glare disapprovingly at Nick. 'And *he* assaulted you again.'

'Looked mutual to me,' Leon declared, turning an arch look on Sue. 'Trying to work damages on this score is not going to wear. She was certainly not fighting, not the slightest sign of struggle. In fact...'

'Do you mind?' Nick cut in. 'This is my private office.'

'Which happens to be for work, Nick,' came the fast and pointed retort. 'Remember work? What we're supposed to be doing here?'

'And I see the delivery has been made,' Sue said, expressing equal disapproval of the current use of Nick's office. 'Come on, Barbie. You're leaving with me.'

'Barbie...'

Nick's softly musing repetition of her name

squeezed her heart. She couldn't let him start thinking about it, possibly making the connection to the girl he'd known when they'd shared the same neighbourhood.

'It's Sue's nickname for me,' she blurted out, feverishly seeking some meaning for it as he looked quizzically at her. 'Like barbed wire. I'm usually very prickly with men who come on to me.'

'And you should be prickly with this one, too,' Sue strongly advised, ever sharp at picking up the ball. 'He's not just coming on. He's charging.'

Nick ignored this remark, ignored both Leon and Sue, focusing entirely on Barbie, his vivid blue eyes eloquently pleading the cause of a here-and-now involvement which he wanted to stretch beyond this moment. To her intense relief, there was no flash of memory clouding that desire, nothing but the need to know, the need to reach out and hold on.

'So what is your real name?' he asked.

Her mind whirled, groping for an answer. She was christened Barbara Anne. Her second name should be easy to remember.

'Anne,' she replied. But what about a surname? Lamb was a dead giveaway. 'Shepherd,' she added, the sheep association popping out. 'Anne Shepherd.'

He smiled both encouragement and satisfaction in her conceding it to him. 'So now we're properly introduced.' And his voice was like warm velvet, caressing her.

'Right!' Leon snapped. 'Having got that settled...'

'Butt out, Leon. I have more to settle.' Nick's expression changed to one of powerful intent as he looked at his partner and Sue beside him. 'If you'd be so kind as to leave us alone for a few minutes...'

'Fine!' Leon agreed on a huff.

'I'll wait in reception,' Sue instructed, giving Barbie a look that asked if she had a hole in her head.

And Barbie briefly wondered if she did as they left, closing the door behind them. Then Nick was turning back to her, lifting the arm he'd freed, tenderly stroking her cheek, her hair, his eyes telling her how very desirable he found the woman she now was. It was like champagne bubbling through her blood, too wonderfully intoxicating to dilute it with any bitter dregs from the past.

'Meet me after work. We'll have dinner together. Is that possible?'

'Where?'

'Where do you live?'

That was tricky with Sue all too ready to mouth off. If she was to keep her real identity a secret—and that was paramount right now—best to keep Nick away from their apartment in Ryde.

'I'll meet you in the city,' she said, showing a reservation about accepting too much too fast.

He didn't argue. He smiled reassurance, probably remembering her claim to *prickliness*. 'Whatever you wish. Do you know the restaurant, Pier Twenty-One, at Circular Quay?'

'I'll find it.'

'Seven o'clock?'

'Yes.'

'You won't disappear on me again?'

'I'll meet you for dinner.'

No promises beyond that, Barbie told herself. She may have embarked on madness, but she could allow this much time with Nick, just to see...

'I'll look forward to it,' he said, a happy grin spreading across his handsome face as he released her and withdrew her sunglasses from his shirt pocket. 'No more disguises?'

Barbie flushed, the deception she was determinedly playing very high on her awareness scale. 'It was my job,' she excused.

'I'd like to hear more about that tonight.' He gave her the glasses then stepped away to scoop up her hat from the floor. 'Sorry about this but I had to take it off,' he said, smiling a rueful apology as he handed it back to her. 'Your hair is too beautiful to hide.'

She was hiding much more than her hair, Barbie thought, as she crammed the hat on. This was a game—a dangerous game—of hide-and-seek. If and when she was caught...would she know how to handle it by then?

'Thank you,' she said. 'I must go now. Sue's waiting.'

'Is she your boss?'

'More a case of mutual interests,' Barbie answered evasively.

He didn't pursue the point. 'Until tonight then,' he said, ushering her to the door.

Just before Barbie made her exit, her gaze flicked

to the broken fairy wings, propped against the file cabinet.

Were they both pursuing a fantasy?

She paused in the opened doorway to take one last direct look at him and was instantly swamped by the sexual awareness he generated. His eyes blazed with a wanting that had nothing to do with fantasy, and her whole body sizzled with a response that was very very real.

'Tonight,' he repeated.

It was like a drumbeat on her heart.

She nodded and left, unable to think, just feeling...feeling what Nick Armstrong did to her...not wanting to let it go.

CHAPTER SIX

'ANNE SHEPHERD?'

Barbie sighed at the caustic drawl from Sue. At least they were out of the renovated warehouse which held the various departments of Multi-Media Promotions, and in the privacy of their own company car. She had known Sue wouldn't hold her tongue for long, but she wasn't ready to answer. She didn't want to explain anything.

How could anyone really explain *feelings?*

'Come on, Barbie. This is going a bit far, isn't it?'

The critical comment stung, yet Barbie hastily reasoned Sue didn't—couldn't—understand how this new thing between her and Nick would be spoiled if the truth of her identity was known. She just wanted to let it run for a while, without those shadows from the past.

The past of Sydney was all around her in this old inner city suburb of Glebe where Nick had his business offices. She stared out at the terrace houses, many of them turned into trendy restaurants and galleries now. Times changed, places changed, people changed. Or at least their views did. Nick definitely saw her differently, very positively *wanting* her in his life.

'A false name,' Sue scorned. 'How long do you think you can fool him with it?'

'Long enough,' Barbie muttered.

'Enough for what?'

'Never mind.'

'If this is an extension of the revenge idea, you're playing with real fire, Barbie, and you may get badly burned,' Sue warned. 'Saturday night's act was harmless, good for your pride, but if you're planning on a closer encounter...'

'It's not revenge.'

This terse statement of fact hung in the silence between them as Sue drove the length of the Anzac Bridge and took the route towards Ryde. Wanting to smooth over the ruction in their usual good understanding, Barbie offered the one piece of proof that Nick was not a shallow rat.

'He bought the fabric to mend my fairy wings.'

It was answered with blistering scepticism. 'Leverage. The guy will try anything to get to you. And he has, hasn't he? I'll bet you right now nothing more will be done about mending those wings, because he's already won what he wanted.'

There was no reply to that argument. Only time would tell the truth of it.

'What's the next step?' Sue went on relentlessly. 'Dinner, bed and breakfast?'

Barbie grimaced over the derision, but at this point she no longer cared what Sue thought. 'Dinner. This evening,' she answered. 'I'll be meeting him in the city so I'll need the car if that's okay with you.'

'Dinner,' Sue muttered, shooting a dark look of warning as she added, 'Well don't kid yourself that wolf hasn't got bed and breakfast on the agenda.'

Barbie's chin lifted, defying the bloom of heat in her cheeks. 'So what if he has? I might want that, too. You said yourself I should get him out of my system.'

'Not this way, Barbie.'

'You opened this can of worms, insisting we needed the business. The lid won't go back on it now. I've always wanted him, Sue. That's the truth of it.'

'You're pursuing a dream.'

'Yes. Why not?'

'Starting it off on a lie, Barbie? Deceiving him as to who you are?'

'A name doesn't mean anything. It's the person who counts.'

'If it doesn't *mean* anything, why hide it?'

Barbie once again retreated into silence, hating the argument, not wanting to listen to her friend. It was *her* business, not Sue's. She was the one whose childhood and teenage years were emotionally entangled with Nick Armstrong.

Once those memories were triggered in Nick, she would shrivel inside and all the good feelings would die. He would look at her and see *Baa-Baa*. Whereas if they connected really well as the people they were today, perhaps they might reach a point where they could both laugh over those old memories.

'Do you expect me to back you up?'

Hearing the strong disapproval in Sue's voice, Barbie had no hesitation in releasing her friend from any responsibility for whatever ensued from this decision. 'No, I don't. Thanks for not blowing my cover back there in Nick's office. From now on I'll do my best to keep you right out of it. It's my play.'

'A bit difficult when Leon has asked me out.'

'What?' Barbie gaped at her in surprise, not for a moment having anticipated this outcome.

Sue shrugged. 'I like him. He's fun. He's invited me to a party this coming Saturday night.'

Barbie sagged back into her passenger seat, closed her eyes and rubbed her forehead, needing to still the whirl of complications that this connection set off in her mind. Leon Webster had been a friend of Nick's since university days, and shared the same business. They were bound to talk together as much as she and Sue did. Impossible to ask Sue to drop him if she liked him. That wasn't fair.

'We'll have to keep these involvements separate,' she argued. 'You with Leon. Me with Nick.'

'Or you could be honest with him. Get it out of the way,' came the salutory retort.

'No. Not yet.'

'I don't want to lie to Leon about you, Barbie.'

'Then don't. Do what you have to do and let me do what I have to do. Okay?'

Sue didn't reply. She didn't say anything more on the subject. Neither did Barbie. But they were both very conscious of the serious difference of opinion between them—an unwanted wedge in their long and close friendship.

Was Nick Armstrong worth it?

Barbie grimly decided she would have to find that out, beyond any shadow of a doubt... before Saturday night.

Having explained the circumstances of the *Drop Dead Delivery* to Leon, and the subsequent unmasking of Anne Shepherd, who'd played the fairy princess, Nick felt no compunction to explain anything else. Anne Shepherd was now his business—his personal, private business—and Leon had no rights over it.

'Thank you for being persuasive with Sue Olsen on my behalf,' he said, winding up the inquisition. 'I hope it wasn't too much of a chore. As it is, Anne and I can take it from here so you can drop it, Leon. Okay? Back to work now?'

'No, it's not okay,' came the sharp retort.

'You did remind me when you broke into my office that we were supposed to be working,' Nick dryly pointed out.

'Sue was right. You're charging like a bull, Nick. I bet you've got Anne lined up to race her off to bed tonight.'

Not *race*. He wanted to savour and revel in every bit of anticipation, then eke out every bit of pleasure he knew was coming with his fairy princess. Impossible to explain how he felt about her to Leon.

'I'm not working tonight so it's no concern of yours,' he said dismissively.

'No concern!' Leon rose from his chair with the rising of his voice, hurling his arms around and ges-

ticulating dramatically as he paced around the office,
flinging out a torrent of unsolicited advice. 'So I'm
supposed to ignore it while you get into another mess
with a woman. Remember, Tanya? You raced her off
to bed the first night you met her, then spent the next
four months finding out what a bitch she was. You're
too fast on the draw, Nick.'

This was different. No way was Anne Shepherd in
the same ring as Tanya Wells and he didn't like Leon
linking them, either. Irritated by his friend's criticism
he shot him a quelling glare. 'Look who's talking?'

'Sure I've done it, too,' Leon whipped back. 'Taking what's there whenever I've felt the urge. No harm
done with willing parties. But the break-up with Liz
taught me something. Great sex peters out when you
find you've got nothing in common and you're pulling against each other's interests. Like with you and
Tanya. Right?'

Nick leaned back in his chair and visually quizzed
the reformed character Leon was supposedly dem-
onstrating. 'When did this wisdom descend on you?'
he asked. 'I didn't notice it in play at the party on
Saturday night. Seems to me I remember...'

'There was no one *important* there,' Leon cut in
emphatically. 'You said this Anne Shepherd is important to you.'

'So?'

'So treat her right. Get to know her.'

'I intend to.'

'It didn't look that way to me when Sue and I came

in,' Leon reminded him, sounding like a preacher pushing some righteous path.

Nick frowned at him, wishing he'd mind his own business. 'I appreciate your concern. Now let's drop it, shall we?'

Leon stopped his pacing and took a stand, glaring vexed disapproval. 'She and Sue are friends. Long-time friends. And business partners,' he stated curtly.

'I gathered that.'

'Sue is very protective of her when it comes to pushy guys.'

'I gathered that, too.'

'I like Sue Olsen. She's in tune with me. We might become a big item.'

Understanding dawned. His friend and partner fancied the little redhead. 'Each to his own, Leon.'

The usual agreement between them was not forthcoming. Leon did not relax. If anything, the tension he was emanating increased, his hands clenching and unclenching as though he wanted to throw a punch.

Bemused and rather unsettled by the aggressive flow from his friend, Nick waited to be enlightened further.

'We've got wires crossed here, Nick,' he stated with an underlying throb of vehemence, quite uncharacteristic of his usual easy-going manner. 'I'm counting on you not to give them a negative charge.'

'Right at this moment I don't see any problem,' Nick assured him confidently. All the signals with Anne were very positive.

'Well, think about this.' Leon wagged an admon-

ishing finger. 'Sue wouldn't be so protective of Anne
without a damned good reason. I figure there's some
bad history that might need soothing over. Better find
out what that reason is before you charge, Nick. Or
we may find ourselves in major conflict.'

He made his exit on that sobering challenge, closing the door with a bang that telegraphed very serious
concern.

It gave Nick considerable pause for thought.

Leon must *really* fancy the redhead.

And he was right. There were crossed wires here.

A strong sexual interest could break up friendships.
He'd seen it happen many a time, women coming
between men, men coming between women. It could
mess up family relationships, too, when an interest
wasn't approved, severely testing loyalties.

Nevertheless, he couldn't see why it should happen
here. Sue Olsen had certainly been protective of Anne,
and clearly there was some hurtful history he didn't
know about. The signposts had been spelled out.

Barbie—barbed wire—prickly with men who came
on to her.

But he hadn't *come on to her*. It was she who had
initiated the kiss at his birthday party. And today, she
had known what he was about to do. There'd been no
protest, either verbally or physically. Remembering the
touch of her tongue on his...nothing unwilling about
her desire to taste him, to explore the wild exhilaration
of arousing more and more excitement... Nick felt
himself stirring, needing what she could give him.

There was no doubt in his mind.

She'd wanted to satisfy herself, as much as he'd wanted to satisfy himself.

Mutual wanting.

Where could it go wrong?

CHAPTER SEVEN

'YOUR table, sir.'

'Thank you.'

'And you're to be joined by?'

'I'll see her coming.'

'A drink while you wait, sir?'

'A jug of iced water will be fine.'

'I'll be right back with it.'

The waiter was as good as his promise, bringing the jug and pouring Nick a long glass of iced water before leaving him alone to wait for Anne. Normally he would have ordered a beer to relax over, smoothing away the tensions of the day, but he didn't have work on his mind, and the tension he felt was exciting, not to be diminished.

Tonight of all nights, Nick didn't want his senses blurred by alcohol. He would order wine when Anne came. A glass or two spaced over dinner wouldn't dull his mind from concentrating on everything about her. As he settled back in his chair and looked around him, taking in the colour and movement of the quay, he realised he had never felt so *alive*, waiting for a woman.

A glance at his watch showed it was still five minutes short of seven o'clock. Having reserved this out-of-doors table, under the huge marble colonnade

that led to the opera house, Nick was in the ideal
position to watch for Anne, and he found himself enjoying the passing parade of people and the coming
and going of harbour ferries. Usually he was in too
much of a hurry to take notice of what were familiar
sights but this evening even the air smelled sweeter.

It had been a warm day for mid-November and the
warmth still lingered. With daylight saving in force,
tourists were still milling around, happily clicking
cameras. Theatre-goers in evening dress strolled past,
heading for their choice of entertainment; a concert,
a play, a ballet performance. Nick's interest wasn't
captivated by any of the stylish women. None of them
held a candle to the one he was waiting for.

His wandering gaze picked her out of the promenade of people when she was still some fifty metres
away, coming past the newspaper and magazine stall
that served ferry passengers. His breath caught in his
throat at sight of her. She shone. And the whole scene
he'd been watching receded into grey nothingness.

Her glorious hair was loose, its gleaming mass rippling down over her shoulders. She'd discarded the
black suit, an unpalatable reminder of his aborted relationship with Tanya. The dress she wore was like
the rising sun—pale bands of soft yellow and or-
ange—a clingy, filmy creation that flowed lovingly
over and around her curvy figure and ended in a fluid
flare well above her knees. A creamy wrap hung
around her arms. A small gold bag dangled from one
hand and at the end of her long golden-tanned legs
flashed cream-and-gold sandals.

She was beautiful, utterly, heart-mashingly beautiful. She was also so vibrantly *female,* every sexual instinct in Nick started sizzling, demanding primal satisfaction. He rose from his chair with the mindless speed of a lemming rushing towards a cliff, and barely stopped himself from striding out to sweep her into his arms.

Charging like a bull...

Leon's warning punched through the body grip of desire. Nick forced himself to relax. Take the time to get to know her, he sternly told himself. It was important. Yet everything within him screamed it didn't matter. Only this feeling mattered.

The abrupt movement of a man standing up from one of the tables outside the Pier Twenty-One restaurant instantly caught Barbie's eye. Her heart flipped. It was Nick. Nick, waiting for her, watching her come to him.

Keep walking, she fiercely told herself, determined not to let her feet falter, thereby revealing some uncertainty about a meeting which should seem perfectly welcome to a woman who was attracted to a man. She should look eager, pleased to find him waiting for her. Anne Shepherd would. It was the sixteen-year-old Barbie Lamb who shrank from facing him.

But this was nine years down the track.

Barbie had the eerie sensation of a tunnel opening up between them, with Nick Armstrong at the other end of it, a powerful magnet tugging on the woman she was now, tugging inexorably on the most primitive depths of her sexuality, arousing needs that confused any sense of romance she'd ever had.

The bustle of people around her faded from her consciousness. It was as though only she and Nick were real. Nothing else mattered. She wasn't even aware of her legs moving anymore, only of getting closer and closer to him, her whole body zinging in anticipation of making contact.

He had changed out of his business suit. He wore an open-necked dark red shirt with black trousers and somehow the more casual clothes amplified his very male physique, projecting a dangerous dominance that both thrilled her and stirred a tremulous vulnerability. She dragged her gaze back to his face, the darkly handsome face that had haunted many dreams. He smiled at her and it was like a burst of sunshine chasing away the miseries of the past.

I'm Anne, she thought, and smiled back at him... Anne Shepherd, letting the ghost of a broken young heart melt away under the brilliance of being smiled upon.

He stepped around the table and pulled out a chair ready for her, a gentlemanly courtesy that was all too frequently overlooked these days in the dubious name of equality. 'You look wonderful,' he said, his voice slightly furred, sending a sensual shiver down her spine.

'Thank you,' she replied, her mind too fuzzy with pleasure to produce any other words.

He gestured to the chair and she sat, helping him adjust its position for comfortable access to the table.

He hadn't offered his hand in greeting—no body contact at all—yet his closeness behind her emanated a warmth that seemed to stroke her skin and he lingered there for moments after she was settled.

Was she imagining it or was he touching her hair? Perhaps the light breeze off the harbour was ruffling it. Yet her pulse quickened at the thought of him feeling it, liking it, wanting to touch.

She was about to look up when he moved, stepping around the table, back to his own chair. His smile seemed to simmer with sensual satisfaction as he sat down and Barbie was instantly certain he had run his fingers through her hair.

'It's a lovely evening,' she remarked, trying to ignore the wild catapulting of her heart inside her chest.

'Perfect,' he answered, his vivid blue eyes focused directly on her, making the comment intensely personal.

'Is this a favourite restaurant of yours?'

'It's good and it's handy. I live close by.'

'Oh?' Her stomach fluttered. Was Sue right about bed and breakfast being on his agenda? For all her bravado about possibly wanting that, too…did she really? This fast?

He gave her a quizzical look. 'Does that disturb you?'

She shrugged. 'Why should it? You have to live somewhere. Though it must be expensive to rent anything in this part of the city.'

'I don't rent. I bought one of the apartments built above the colonnade.'

'*This* colonnade?'

Impossible to hide her shock. She remembered his family being financially sound—a large, double-storeyed brick home at Wamberal, two not overly expensive cars, living well and wanting for nothing—but she'd never thought of them as in the millionaire class. To own an apartment at Benelong Point, overlooking the harbour…had Nick achieved so much in partnership with Leon Webster?

He frowned. 'It *does* disturb you.'

'It's just…you're talking very serious money here. I didn't realise…' The party on Observatory Hill should have told her. Plus the renovated warehouse at Glebe. Did he own that, too?

'Realise what?'

'How…how rich you are,' she blurted out.

His mouth quirked. 'Is that a black mark against me?'

It sounded absurd. How could wealth attained by hard work and talent be a black mark against anyone? Yet it put him on a level far above her own situation where she and Sue were struggling to make ends meet. She wondered who and what Tanya Wells was—a high-flying career person, a socialite?

All this time she'd been thinking of Nick as the Nick she had known, wanting him to love her, while he…how was he thinking of her? Bed and breakfast?

'What's the problem, Anne?' he asked quietly, caringly.

Anne…

She had changed from the person she once was.

He had changed, too.

This was, indeed, a new ball game, and it had to be accepted as the current day reality it was. Pursuing a dream—an old dream—suddenly seemed very foolish. Yet looking at Nick, she felt the same drawing power he'd always had on her. More...

She took a deep breath and spelled out one undeniable truth. 'I'm not in your league. I'm a professional singer but it's never been what I'd call steady work and I've never cracked the big time. I love singing and I make a living out of it.'

'Nothing wrong with that,' he slid in. 'Not many people can make a living out of doing what they really enjoy doing. It's great that you've been able to in what must be a tough, competitive field.' He leaned forward earnestly, his eyes warmly approving. 'I admire you for going after it, taking it on.'

Smooth words, persuasive words...sincere words?

'I share the rent for a very ordinary, two-bedroom apartment at Ryde. Hardly high class,' she stated brusquely, needing to clear up this issue of status.

He smiled ironically. 'When I first came to Sydney, I rented a room in a dump of a place at Surrey Hills. It was all I could afford. I do understand living within one's means, Anne. And I respect it.'

'But it's different for you now, and you're obviously accustomed to its being different,' she argued.

'Yes. And I won't say I'm not glad to be in a position where I can buy most things I want.'

Did he think he could buy her?

Had his money attracted Tanya Wells?

'*Things,* Anne,' he went on, a more urgent intensity in his voice. 'Like having dinner here whenever I want to. Driving a classy car. Taking a trip overseas. Living in luxury. And all of that is good. I like it. But it doesn't answer all the needs I have.'

His eyes burned into hers as he asked, 'Would it answer all yours?'

She flushed. 'I'm not a gold-digger.'

'And I'm not looking for a cheap thrill from you.'

'What *do* you want with me?' The challenge sliced off her tongue, laced with the cynicism Sue had fed her.

'To know you.'

'There are all sorts of *knowing,*' she flashed back, her eyes nailing her meaning. 'What sense are you talking about?'

'Every sense.'

She stared at him, desperate to believe he spoke the truth. He held her gaze unflinchingly, beating down any scepticism over his intentions. The tightness in her chest slowly eased. Sue had to be wrong. Nick looked truly genuine in his desire to know more of her than a one-night stand would give him.

'Did some rich guy hurt you, Anne?' he asked quietly.

Again she flushed under his directness. 'Why would you think so?'

'Firstly, you are quite stunningly beautiful. Having you would be an ego boost to many men, and rich guys generally see beauty in a woman as a reflection of their success in life.'

'Do you?'

He shook his head. 'I want more in a woman than skin-deep beauty. I guess you could say I've been taken in by that a couple of times,' he added wryly. 'We all make mistakes. I was just wondering if you'd been taken in, too. It was the idea of my being rich that upset you.'

Her hands fluttered an agitated appeal. 'I hadn't thought about you in those terms. It came as a shock. I felt...foolish.'

He reached across the table and took one of her hands, pressing it into a stillness that was meant to soothe fears, yet the feel of his flesh encasing hers sent a wave of exhilarating warmth through her bloodstream and set off deep tremors of desire for a more intimate touching.

'Give us a chance, Anne. You and me. Is that asking too much?'

'No,' she whispered, barely able to catch her breath. He was gently stroking her palm with his thumb, sparking off electric tingles. The effect was mesmerising. She couldn't shake her mind free of it.

His whole expression emanated a fervent need to convince as he said, 'I feel...'

A waiter interrupted, offering them menus. The moment was lost and Barbie could barely curb her frustration, sensing Nick had been about to reveal something important to her. As it was, he withdrew his hand and turned his attention to the waiter, who proceeded to rattle off 'The Specials' for tonight.

She was too distracted to hear them properly and

when Nick asked, 'Do you fancy any of those?' she had to ask the waiter to go through them again.

Even then the food combinations he listed were confusing, unfamiliar. Haute cuisine had not featured largely in her life. Fashionable restaurants like this one were too expensive and she'd never had the time to take an interest in fancy cooking. Rather than reveal her ignorance, she looked to Nick for help.

'What do you recommend?'

'Do you like seafood?'

'Love it.'

'The barbecued calamari in oregano, coriander and lime, and the sole grilled with lemon grass butter are both excellent here.'

He rattled them off, obviously having no problem at all in remembering the ingredients and accepting them as a good mixture without question. He also clearly expected her to choose a starter and a main meal, regardless of cost.

'Is that what you're having?' she checked.

'Yes.'

'Then I'll have it, too.' She just hoped the herbs and lemon grass stuff didn't turn her stomach.

'Wine, sir?'

'The Brown Brothers Chardonnay,' Nick answered without even glancing at the wine list. He smiled at Barbie. 'If that's all right with you.'

'Fine,' she quickly replied, though the Brown Brothers were a complete mystery to her. She and Sue bought wine in a cask from the supermarket. 'I won't be drinking much,' she warned. 'I'm driving.'

'I understand,' he replied, not voicing even the slightest protest or showing a trace of frustration.

Which relieved Barbie's inner turmoil over the bed and breakfast agenda. If seduction had been on Nick's mind, he would surely have said something like, 'A glass or two won't hurt.'

The waiter collected the menus they hadn't even glanced at, and departed, leaving them to themselves again. Relieved to have the meal-ordering over and done with, Barbie could once more think about what had transpired before the interruption.

She wished she could ask Nick what it was *he felt,* but decided it was up to him to continue the conversation. It might appear too forward, too *anxious,* to pursue it herself.

'Would you like some iced water?' he asked, picking up the jug on the table.

'Yes, please.'

He filled a glass for her, adding to the impression he would respect her wishes about the wine-drinking and not try to push her into doing anything she didn't really want. It served to make Barbie feel more comfortable with the situation, certainly less tense about his motives for pursuing a relationship with her.

They sat back, studying each other, assessing where they were now. Nick looked satisfied, content for them simply to be together like this. He wore self-assurance as though it were ingrained, which it probably was, given the success he'd made of his business.

Maybe he'd always had it, an innate part of his character, Barbie thought, remembering how he'd been a natural leader even when they were children in the old Wamberal neighbourhood. Everyone had taken notice of what Nick suggested, what Nick decided, what Nick did. He created games. He was clever and brave and exciting to be with.

Was this just another exciting game to him?

Give us a chance. You and me.

It was silly to let doubts and fears get in the way.

You and me… magic words.

Even this much was a wish come true. She had to try for more, wherever it led.

Occupied with her inner thoughts, she hadn't noticed his expression change until he spoke. His words instantly shattered any peace of mind Barbie had attained.

'You remind me of someone I once knew.'

Light, musing words, but she caught the tension in his stillness, the concentrated weighing in his eyes, and an iron fist squeezed her heart.

CHAPTER EIGHT

NICK saw the shock hit her…the tightening of her face, the flare of angst in her eyes, the swift struggle for control…and any possible doubt was wiped from his mind.

Anne Shepherd *was* Barbie Lamb.

He should have put it together sooner—the deep-down sense of knowing her, the physical instincts she triggered, the intensity of feeling she projected, the passion, Sue Olsen calling her Barbie.

The passage of so many years had pushed his memory of her into the far background and the physical changes wrought by those same years had dazzled his vision. On top of which, the circumstances of their meeting again hadn't helped him see straight. But he was seeing straight now and he knew he was about to walk a tightrope where the wrong step might well mean death to any hope of the relationship he wanted with her.

He had to know what she was thinking, feeling, whether he had a real chance with her. *Bad history,* Leon had said, and he'd been spot-on. Except the bad history, in this case, was personal to him, not some anonymous rich guy. *He* was the one who had inflicted the hurt that needed soothing.

Her lashes swept down, veiling her telltale eyes as

85

she leaned forward and picked up her glass of water, playing for time, struggling for composure. Her hand shook, lifting the glass to her lips. He watched the convulsive movement of her throat as she sipped, and knew she felt sick, as sick as he did at what he had done to her, while telling himself it was for the best.

He didn't need to be told why she'd played the fairy princess as she had to him...the burning desire to interest and excite, to make him wish for what he had rejected, to tantalise him with the promise of it, then walk away. Was tonight about teasing him more before she slapped him in the face with it? When she put that glass down, would she be Barbie Lamb or Anne Shepherd?

Barbie sipped the iced water, using the glass to hide her face and its contents to cool the fever of uncertainties that gripped her. Was he beginning to recognise her? Reminding him of someone was not positive identification, she sternly told herself, forcing down the sick, panicky feeling. It might not be Barbie Lamb he was thinking of at all.

Everything within her recoiled from confronting the past. Not yet, her heart screamed. She couldn't bear it. She had to have this chance with him, free and clear of spoiling memories. Play for more time, need dictated. He couldn't know for certain who she was.

Feeling slightly more composed, she lowered the glass and attempted a wry little smile. 'I'm not sure any woman likes to be told that.'

He was silent for a moment, seemingly slow in digesting the comment. Her nerves jangled, fear whispering he'd been waiting for some admission. Then to her intense relief he laughed and shook his head. He leaned forward, resting his forearms on the table, his eyes bathing her with warm reassurance as he answered her.

'I wasn't comparing. You shine alone, Anne. Believe me, I feel incredibly lucky that our paths have crossed.'

The fear of recognition receded. Her smile relaxed into pleasure at his compliment. 'Then how do I remind you of someone?' she teased, confident now that he hadn't made the connection.

'It's the eyes,' he said, nodding in confirmation of his observation as he looked directly at them. 'Such a clear light grey. Mostly there's a bit of blue or brown—hazel. I've only seen eyes like yours once before.'

Hers? Had he ever really noticed them back then? The need to know forced the question. 'So who shares them with me?'

He shrugged dismissively. 'It was a long time ago. The memory just struck me. Where I grew up, there were lots of kids in the neighbourhood and we hung around together. One of the girls had eyes like yours.'

That girl was me! she almost screamed at him. It was a struggle to contain the sudden violent surge of emotion as the hurt of being referred to as just a girl in a neighbourhood gang seared every bit of common sense in her brain.

A wise person would probably let the matter drop, move on. After all, there was nothing to be gained by raking over the past and much to lose. Anne Shepherd was not *one of the girls*. She shone alone in Nick Armstrong's eyes.

But an old, old devil of torment writhed inside her, insisting on some release. The opening was there to probe exactly what Nick had thought of her in those days, without him even suspecting who she was. Painful it might be, but she couldn't let it go. The words tripped out, taking a dangerous path that was loaded with pitfalls.

'You must have a very clear memory of this girl. Was she special in some way?'

He smiled reminiscently. 'Yes, she was. It didn't matter how often the guys tried to chase her off, she determinedly stuck to joining in whatever we did, regardless of how tough the challenge was. She wouldn't get left behind and never once cried or complained if she got hurt in the process. She followed us everywhere.'

Baa-Baa Lamb.

Her chest tightened. Still she persisted on the path of knowledge, recklessly bent on filling out the picture of Nick's memory of her.

'Did you find her a pest?'

'No.' His expression became more seriously reflective. 'It's strange, looking back. She was fearless. Yet there was a terrible innocence in her fearlessness. She made me want to protect her.'

'I can't imagine the character you've drawn would want protecting.'

His eyes flicked appreciation of her understanding. 'You're right. She had a fierce pride. But I was five years older so a certain weight of responsibility fell to me.'

'Why to you?'

'I guess because...' His mouth twisted with irony. '...she looked to me. Rightly or wrongly I felt I was the one influencing her.' He paused before quietly adding, 'In the end I had to stop it.'

Barbie's mind staggered at this totally unexpected admission of a *deliberate* act of rejection, a weighing of the situation she had never ever suspected. The question tumbled out, impossible to hold back.

'Why?'

'It became too personal.'

The provocative reply goaded her into pursuing the point. 'How too personal?'

He made a rueful grimace. 'She didn't even see that my younger brother, who was more her age, had a crush on her.'

Barbie's mind reeled. Danny? Shy Danny with the stutter who had never discussed anything but school-work with her? She'd always tried to be kind to him, mostly because he was Nick's brother, but she'd never thought of him as anything else but Nick's brother.

'Are you saying she saw only you?'

'Something like that. It upset Danny. He'd rage at me...but I hadn't made any moves on her. She was

too young for me anyway. It would have been wrong
all around.'

'So how did you put a stop to it?'

He sighed. 'I made it obvious I was attracted to
someone else.'

'Were you?'

'Enough to make it stick. It got Danny off my
back.'

'And the girl? It got *her* off your back, too?' Again
the question tumbled out, on a rush of bitterness this
time, and she could only hope he didn't notice a
change in her tone.

For a moment there was a pained expression in his
eyes and Barbie registered that he took no pleasure
in the success of his manoeuvre. 'It was effective in
that sense,' he acknowledged. 'But she didn't take up
with Danny. I didn't think she would. She simply
dropped out of our lives, kept to herself. A year or so
later, her family moved away, up the coast somewhere, Byron Bay, I think.'

'But you still remember her…very clearly,' Barbie
commented, hiding the terrible twist of irony in her
heart.

'She was part of a big chunk of my life.' His eyes
warmly invited *her* memories as he said, 'You must
have had people in your growing-up years who coloured your life, one way or another.'

He'd coloured it black. Totally black in that act of
rejection. Only now did she realise there had been
greys. He hadn't been a shallow rat. He'd cared about

his brother's feelings… Danny, who'd meant nothing to her…

'Where does your family live, Anne?' Nick prompted.

She shook herself out of the dark reverie brought on by these revelations. Later she would think about them, put them in perspective. Dealing with *now* had to take priority. She had Nick here with her and she didn't want to lose what might be between them this time.

'Queensland. On the Sunshine Coast,' she answered truthfully. Her parents had moved on from Byron Bay.

'You're a long way from home.'

'I've been travelling around the country since I was eighteen. Pursuing a career in singing meant I had to.'

He smiled his understanding. 'Of course.'

'What about your family?' It was less dangerous ground.

'My parents still live at Wamberal. That's on the Central Coast.'

So nothing had changed there.

'The rest of the family has scattered,' he went on. 'I have a sister who lives in Sydney. She's married and has a couple of children.'

Carole…two years older than Barbie and very fashion-conscious from the moment she hit her teen years. It was a safe bet she'd married well. 'And your brother…the one you've mentioned?' she pressed.

'He's currently in San Diego. Danny is into yacht racing. He always was mad about boats.'

She remembered the small catamaran the Armstrongs had owned, Danny sailing it on Wamberal Lake. He'd asked her to go with him and she had a couple of times, more to show she was game for the experience than to share it with Danny. She'd really wanted to sail with Nick.

It was good to hear Danny was so far away and mad about something else. At least he couldn't interfere with this relationship.

Three waiters descended on them, one with the bottle of wine, another offering a selection of bread rolls from a basket, the third setting down the calamari starter. Barbie was grateful for the little flurry of activity which took Nick's focus away from her. She hadn't realised how difficult it would be, pretending to be a stranger, carrying the emotional strain of monitoring every word she said, trying to make her questions sound like natural curiosity.

She took a bread roll, smiled at the food waiter who said, 'Enjoy!' nodded to the wine waiter who held the bottle hovered inquiringly over her glass. By the time all the business of serving was done, she had almost convinced herself Nick could not be blamed for the decision he'd made to *end it,* although it was impossible to end *feelings.* They might be buried, twisted, transformed, but they didn't end.

At least his memories of her held some admiration, mixed with the conflict his brother had caused. Perhaps some regret, too, for what had been lost in the action he had taken. Nevertheless, she didn't want to revisit that old humiliation by talking about it openly. She needed the balm of his current admiration to heal that re-opened wound.

'Something wrong?'

Nick's query jolted her gaze back to his. 'No. Why?' she spilled out, hoping he hadn't sensed any disturbance in her thoughts.

'You seemed to be looking dubiously at the calamari. Would you like to order something else?'

'No. It's just that I've never seen it presented like this.' She smiled to alleviate any concern. 'It's so artistic it's almost a shame to dig into it.'

He picked up his cutlery to encourage her. *'Bon appetit.'*

She followed suit and began to eat, concentrating on the taste of the food, finding the calamari beautifully tender and the subtle flavourings interesting.

Nick's mind was in hyper-drive, trying to assess what was going on in Barbie's head. And heart. She was still sticking to Anne Shepherd. He had no idea if the answers he'd given to her quiz on the past had satisfied her quest to know how he remembered her and what had driven his actions. He could only hope she now understood there had been mitigating circumstances to the denial he'd chosen.

She was the one choosing denial now, he realised, and if he was to have any chance with her, he had to respect her choice. She didn't want to tell her side.

Too hurtful? Too revealing? Would it make her feel too vulnerable?

Which led him to ponder protection. She had thought herself protected today when she'd come to his office. And Anne Shepherd was now protecting the girl he had once known. But was it protection...or deliberate deception feeding a deep, vengeful streak that would lash out at him when she judged *he* was at his most vulnerable?

He instinctively recoiled from this scenario. It was too dark, suggestive of a more disturbed mind than he cared to deal with. Nine years had gone by. He could understand her being wary of him, wary of letting herself be attracted to him, but to deliberately set him up for a fall at this point...no, he didn't want to believe that.

The Barbie Lamb he remembered had been straight and true in everything she'd done. People's characters didn't change. Pride might make her cover up the past, but he was sure there'd been nothing false in her response to his kisses. No pretence. No deception. It had been too real, too giving of herself to the passion that had exploded between them.

Mutual desire.

Or was he fooling himself?

She put down her knife and fork and smiled warmly at him. 'That was delicious. A great recommendation. Thank you.'

An electric charge hit his groin.

'Glad you enjoyed it,' he returned just as warmly, any concern about her motives totally obliterated.

He *wanted* her, regardless of what she called herself, regardless of where the wanting led. He was not about to let this feeling go. Not about to let her go, either.

CHAPTER NINE

His smile made Barbie tingle all over. Even when she was young it had invariably made her feel happy, generating bubbles of joy through her whole bloodstream. Then it had seemed to say he really liked her. And perhaps he had, although other things had been more important to him.

Focused on her now, a woman who was not too young for him, it had a far more powerful impact, loaded with the message he found her infinitely desirable and emanating an intense level of sexual intimacy, his eyes reflecting the knowledge of how she'd felt in his arms, how her mouth had moved with his, and the wanting to savour the experience again and again.

She found herself squeezing her thighs together, capturing and enclosing the excitement he stirred. Her nipples were tightening into hard little buds. Never had she reacted so physically to a man before and she marvelled at the difference between wanting someone from afar and having the desire actively returned at close quarters.

What would have happened if he'd looked at her like this when she was sixteen...if he'd kissed her...?

Barbie shook her head. She had to stop thinking about *then*.

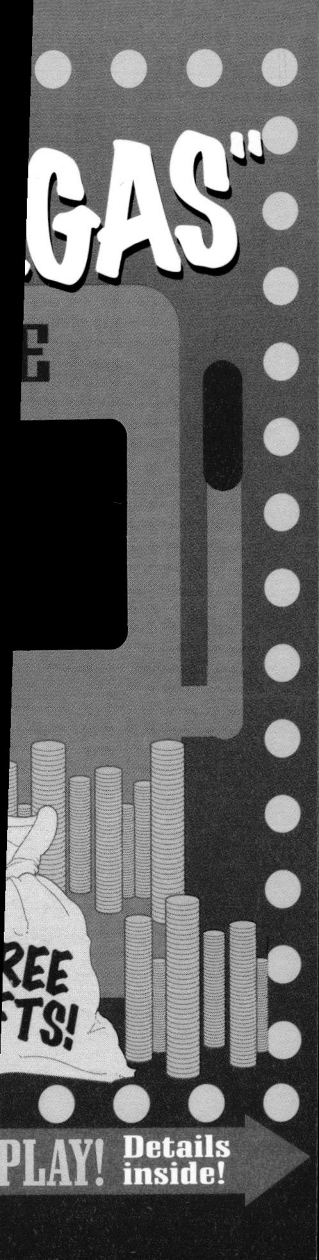
GAS"
PLAY!
Details inside!

Play the

"LAS

3 FRE

FREE GIFTS!

1. Pull back all 3 tabs on th
   see what we have for you
   FREE!

2. Send back this card and y
   novels. These books have
   $4.50 each in Canada, bu

3. There's no catch. You're
   nothing — ZERO — for y
   any minimum number of

4. The fact is, thousands of r
   the Harlequin Reader Serv
   delivery...they like getting
   they're available in stores.
   featuring author news, hor

5. We hope that after receivin
   subscriber. But the choice
   all! So why not take us up
   You'll be glad you did!

FREE!
No Obligation to Buy!
No Purchase Necessary!

Play the
"LAS VEGAS"
Game

YES! I have pulled back the 3 tabs. Please send me all the free Harlequin Presents® books and the gift for which I qualify. I understand that I am under no obligation to purchase any books, as explained on the back and opposite page.

306 HDL DC4S

106 HDL DC4J
(H-P-0S-05/01)

NAME   (PLEASE PRINT CLEARLY)

ADDRESS

APT.#   CITY

STATE/PROV.   ZIP/POSTAL CODE

7 7 7   **GET 2 FREE BOOKS & A FREE MYSTERY GIFT!**

🍀🍀🍀   **GET 2 FREE BOOKS!**

🍒🍒🍒   **GET 1 FREE BOOK!**

🔔🔔🔔   **TRY AGAIN!**

DETACH AND MAIL TODAY ▼

'What's going through your mind?' Nick asked.

'I'm amazed that here we are…you and me,' she answered with more truth than he could possibly know.

'Fate smiled on us, bringing us together.'

She laughed. 'Do you really believe in Fate?'

He shrugged, smiling whimsically. 'Fortuitous circumstances are sometimes uncanny, things falling into place at the right time. Who knows how that works? Is it blind luck or are there energy forces that somehow guide meetings and outcomes?' He paused, his eyes probing hers very personally. 'Perhaps we were always meant to be here at this time and place…you and I.'

Goose bumps ran over her skin at the suggestion of something preordained. 'I could have said no to your invitation.'

'But you didn't.'

The pull had been too great to resist, Barbie silently acknowledged.

He didn't wait for a reply. His eyes still engaging hers with compelling intensity, he softly stated, 'I have the strong sense that I've been waiting for you a very long time.'

It hit a chord that throbbed painfully. He could have found her if he'd wanted to. Though he didn't know who she was, reason dictated, flooding her with confused emotions. Should she tell him now, have it out in the open? And see his expression change to one of shock, embarrassment?

No. She didn't want that.

'Perhaps we were connected in some previous life,' she said with considerable irony.

'And something drove us apart,' he added, his eyes glittering in a way that made her feel uneasy, as though he could see into her soul.

'A very romantic fantasy,' she remarked dryly, picking up her glass of wine, defensively breaking eye contact with him.

There was a momentary silence. Then he laughed, relaxing the intensity he had built up. 'I guess I like the idea of people getting a second chance. We don't always make the right decisions the first time around.'

'That's true,' she agreed, happy to leave it at that...a second chance. 'Though you must have made a lot of right decisions in your business for it to have gone so well.'

'Oh, Leon and I saw the openings, particularly with the Internet developing so fast,' he answered off-handedly.

She set her glass down and leaned forward, eager to know more of his current life. 'I'm sorry to be so ignorant, but what does Multi-Media Promotions actually do?'

'Every form of advertising. Whatever we win a contract for.'

'You mean you design promotional stuff for other companies.'

He nodded. 'We do our best to present their products in a sales-winning format.'

'Give me an example.'

A waiter arrived to take their empty plates and refill

their glasses. The momentary distraction did not deflect Barbie's intent to understand precisely where Nick was now and how he'd got there. Under her pressing interest, he revealed he was the head designer at the company, responsible for all the artwork they produced for their clients.

This, Barbie, was fascinated to hear, was computer-generated, able to be structurally altered or differently coloured by the stroke of a key. Of course, Nick had been known as a whiz at computers in his school days, but he'd never talked about what he did on them to her. Now it seemed he manipulated this technological world at will.

It was obvious he liked his work, enjoyed the challenge of keeping up what he called street-edge designs, and took immense satisfaction in the results he achieved. She listened to the warm enthusiasm in his voice, the passion for getting everything just right and putting his vision across to others, winning their commitment to his concepts. She felt the inner fire and drive that made him the success he was and knew this was a deep part of his personal magnetism.

He believed in himself.

He was a born leader, the kind of man who forged a path that others followed.

And in her heart of hearts she wished she was attached to it, attached to him. Although she'd only been on the edge of his world in her growing-up years, she'd missed the excitement of it, missed the involvement in something special because he was there, making it happen.

He'd left a hole in her life with his driving her away from him, and the desire to have that hole filled now—filled to overflowing—was so intense, she hung on his every word, drank in his every expression, revelled in his sharing all that he was. In many ways, opening his mind to her like this was more intimate than a kiss. It was an acceptance she was his equal in understanding.

The fish course they'd ordered was set in front of them, interrupting the magical flow of communication. Nick drew back in his seat, offering an apologetic smile. 'I've been talking too much about myself.'

'No,' she quickly denied. 'I wanted to hear.'

He quizzically studied the warm sincerity in her eyes. 'It's hardly your scene.'

'Should I be limited to mine?'

He shook his head. 'It's just that I don't usually talk about my work outside of the office.'

'Then I'm honoured.'

'No. *I* am. You really did want to know.'

'It's a big part of you.'

'Yes. But not a part many people care to understand.'

'You mean…like Tanya.'

She wished the acid little comment unsaid the moment it was out of her mouth. It was stupid to bring that woman up when she was no longer in Nick's life. Yet Barbie could not stifle a welling of resentment at his choice of companion during the long years of supposedly *waiting for her.*

Tanya Wells was a horrible person with a really mean, vicious streak. Surely he should have picked that up in her character, or had the sex been enough for him? Take it while the urge was on and walk away when the physical attraction was whittled away by other differences? Was enjoying a new and exciting sexual partner all he was seeking with her now?

'I realise you have no reason to be impressed by Tanya,' he answered ruefully. 'But she could be fun when she was in a good mood.'

'Fun,' Barbie repeated, thinking fun and games in bed.

'Relief from the pressures of work,' he added.

'Perhaps I shouldn't have brought up the subject of work then.'

'It's different with you,' he assured her, his smile playing its powerful havoc again.

Barbie took a deep breath, picked up her knife and fork and purposefully attacked the sole grilled in lemon grass butter, needing something to settle the flutters of excitement in her stomach.

Different... the word was like a wild intoxicant, making her feel giddy with pleasure. Whatever Nick had shared with Tanya—and other women—didn't matter. After all, she'd tried a few relationships herself, wanting more from them than they'd ever given. Sometimes need drove people into making mistakes. Why blame Nick for his?

This was different.

Their second chance.

And everything within Barbie craved to take it, wherever it led.

Nick ate the fish course mechanically, not even tasting it. That crack about Tanya had suddenly left him with the sense of being on trial and he didn't like it, not one bit. He'd explained why he'd acted as he had in the past. Surely any reasonable person would accept the explanation. He'd given her time to digest it, given her another opening to admit who she was, couching it in words that should have reassured her as to how he felt about meeting her again.

Why had she bypassed it?

What more positive signals could he have given her?

The memory of his twenty-first birthday night started plaguing him—the cut-off night for a too young and innocent Barbie. She'd sung the birthday song as the cake had been carried in, a solo effort his mother had arranged because Barbie had such a sweet, true voice. Except the way she'd sung it…he'd been so discomforted by her obvious feeling for him, when she'd presented him with her gift afterwards, he could hardly bear to accept it, shoving it quickly aside.

Only later did he discover it was a watch, the back of it enscribed so endearingly, it had made him feel rotten, even more so because Jasmine Elliot had also given him a watch which he'd worn that night. It had been an unwitting cruelty to Barbie's feelings, although he had ultimately argued to himself, an effective one in pushing her away from him.

She had been far too young.

It couldn't have worked.

Now was their time.

Or hadn't she ever forgiven him that brutal hurt?

Was she priming him for a fall, in revenge for how he'd dealt with her? The avid interest in his work…was it genuine or a ploy to make the high he'd been riding even higher before she walked away, leaving him as flattened as he must have left her all those years ago?

But she had been too young, damn it!

Whereas now…

He surreptitiously watched her eating the meal he'd ordered, daintily loading her fork, lifting it to her mouth. Her hands were steady—finely shaped, long-fingered hands—and he yearned to have those hands stroking him, softly, sensually, lovingly. Even how she slid the fork into her mouth and out again was intensely sexy, the way her lips closed over it then slowly released it.

Her long lashes veiled her eyes, keeping her thoughts a taunting mystery. Her glorious hair shimmered, a silky flow of temptation that teased his imagination and conjured up erotic fantasies…how it would feel on his pillow, his naked body, brushing over his skin.

She finished the meal, her gaze lifting to his as she set down the cutlery. 'You certainly eat well if you come here often,' she remarked appreciatively. 'That was delicious, Nick.'

Her distinctive grey eyes seemed clear of any artifice, yet she had to be taking him for a ride. Why else would she hide her identity? How long did she intend to string it out? How much would she give before turning her back on him?

'There are many fine restaurants around the quay,' he remarked, smiling as he pushed away from his own emptied plate. 'I'd like to introduce you to all of them.'

She blushed. From guilt or pleasure?

'I'd like that, too,' she said simply, her eyes telling him he was the main attraction, not the food.

It made him burn with a torment he couldn't bear. A wild recklessness seized him, demanding he push her to the limit right now, testing how much she wanted to be with him.

'Do you fancy a sweets course?'

She shook her head. 'I've had enough, thank you.'

'Then let me show you where I live. I'll make you coffee in my apartment.'

Her blush deepened. She stared at him, an agony of indecision in her eyes.

Nick sat still, returning her stare, a relentless challenge beating through him in fierce waves. If her wanting him was real, let her prove it by coming with him. If this was some vengeful game, let her reveal it now, excusing herself from the prospect of being alone together in a private place with the risk of a more dangerous intimacy developing between them.

He might be charging like a bull, but the red rag was out, waving through his mind, and he couldn't ignore it.

'All right,' she said in a breathy little voice.

Relief and excitement brewed a heady cocktail. In coming with him she was giving up a certain control, gambling more than any game-player would. Or was she recklessly upping the stakes, driving the ride higher? Whatever her thinking, the ball was now in his court and he instantly determined on playing it hard.

'Have you had the apartment very long?' she asked.

'Two years.'

'Time enough to make it your home.'

She was curious about him, he realised, wanting to see. Wanting to judge? Putting him on further trial?

'It's furnished to my taste, if that's what you mean,' he answered, wondering if she'd make it into his bedroom, wanting her there, resolved on testing *her* wanting.

'Did you use an interior decorator?'

'No. I looked around, bought what appealed to me.'

She nodded. 'I guess you wanted to please your own artistic eye.'

His heart thudded with the realisation that she understood him even more than Leon did. His friend had declared it a waste of time hunting for furniture. Let the experts do it, was his motto, and Nick couldn't deny they'd done a classy job on Leon's apartment.

Still, he preferred his own. It gave him a deeply personal pleasure, living with his own choices.

'Style isn't so important to me,' he acknowledged. 'I like to feel comfortable.'

And more than anything he wanted to feel comfortable with her—nothing hidden between them. He *would* push her to the limit, force her to reveal what was in her mind.

Their waiter came to whisk away the plates. 'The menu for sweets, sir?'

'No. We're finished here.' He took out his wallet and handed over a credit card. 'The bill, please.'

'Be right back, sir.'

'Some more wine?' he asked, noticing her glass was empty.

'No, thank you.' Her eyes were nervous but there was a hardy glint of determination in them, shining through the flickering uncertainties. She didn't want to back off...yet.

The bottle of chardonnay was still half full. Normally he would ask the waiter to cork it for carrying home, but he didn't care about the waste tonight. Anticipation was a fire in his veins. He could barely wait to touch her.

She picked up her glass of iced water and sipped from it. Were her thoughts feverish? Did they need cooling down? Or was the fire of desire in her veins, too?

Well, he'd soon find out.

The waiter returned with the bill. Nick quickly signed it, slid the copy and his credit card into his wallet, then stood up, burning to move this game onto his ground. Before he could reach her chair it was scraping back. She was on her feet, clutching the little gold handbag. For a tense few moments Nick had the impression she was poised for flight—panic in the air—car keys in her bag, people still around them, safety in numbers.

He picked up her creamy wrap which had fallen onto the back of the chair and draped it around her shoulders. There were goose bumps on her arms. 'Cold?' he murmured.

'A bit.'

The admission was slightly choked, breathy.

'You'll be warm in my apartment,' he promised, lifting her hair out of the wrap to let it swing free, taking the opportunity to run it over his hand, revel in its softness.

Her head jerked slightly, skittishly, but she made no protest at the liberty he was taking. Her shoulders squared. She was not going to back off, not at this point. A surge of triumph sizzled through him. He moved, picking up her hand to draw her with him, lacing his fingers through hers to lock her into *his* game plan.

They fluttered before settling into his grip. He heard her suck in a deep breath as she fell into step at his side. His sense of winning was slightly marred by these poignant little signs of vulnerability. Leon's warning flashed into his mind.

You're too fast on the draw, Nick. Treat her right. Get to know her.

Which was all very fine, Nick thought caustically, if she was treating him right.

She'd made the game, closing doors he'd given her more than one opportunity to open. There could be no real knowing of anyone when deliberate deception was in play. Nick felt he had every right to smash those doors down. He had to know where she was at, where she was coming from, where she wanted to be. There could be no going forward until that was settled and Nick wanted a future with her.

Barbie Lamb...the girl...the woman...lost and found.

Not to be lost again.

Not without a fight.

CHAPTER TEN

'IT'S not far,' Nick said encouragingly.

Barbie's heart was galloping. Sue would undoubtedly say she was mad, accompanying him to his apartment. Too far, too fast. But he was holding her hand, taking her on his path, and she couldn't let go, couldn't break away, however far he intended to take her. The need to hold on to him was more compelling than any common sense arguments about how best to handle relationships.

Besides this was different.

It would be impossible to keep her real identity hidden much longer. Since Nick had said Anne Shepherd shone as a uniquely special woman to him, it seemed paramount to use every possible minute in his company, finding out if he really meant it. Only then would Barbie have the confidence to emerge as one and the same woman.

Seeing the home he'd chosen would also tell her more about him, she reasoned, although reason had little to do with the journey she was now taking. The hand gripping hers was irresistible, its warm, possessive strength belonging to Nick... Nick, wanting her. Never mind for what purpose, or for how long. The wanting felt so good, Barbie would have walked anywhere with him.

'Do you ever cook for yourself?' she asked, trying to sound natural, not so affected by his closeness and the invitation to even more closeness.

'Not much. The occasional breakfast.'

Bed and breakfast...

She clamped down on the spoiling thought, but lost the will to pursue any trivial conversation. The nervous excitement of being with Nick consumed her and his silence seemed to transmit the same inner intensity of feeling...an urgency to be alone with her, only with her.

She had no idea how far they walked along the colonnaded promenade, nor was she aware of anything they passed. It was as though she had stepped into a dream world where wishes could come true, and she refused to consider a reality which might be different.

He steered her through a huge marble archway into a rotunda-like foyer that featured a grand staircase winding upwards.

'Do we climb that?' she asked, her voice echoing around the high emptiness, seeming to emphasise the abrupt cut-off from a public place.

'It only leads to floors of offices,' he answered briefly, drawing her towards an elevator set in the side wall.

The doors slid open the moment he hit the Up button. They stepped inside. Nick produced a security card from his shirt pocket and inserted it into a slot on the control board before pressing the number 8. The action indicated an exclusivity that only the very rich could afford. An eighth-floor apartment, directly overlooking the harbour, would indeed be fairyland for her, Barbie thought.

Would Nick treat her like a princess…or would she be coming down to earth with a thump?

Again she pushed the question aside, determined on following his lead. She recalled him saying he'd felt protective of her, except that had been Barbie, not Anne. All the same, she did instinctively trust him not to do anything she didn't want. If there was any problem it probably lay in her own wanting.

Which hit her forcibly when they emerged from the fast-track elevator and he released her hand to unlock and open the door to his apartment. The loss of that small physical contact with him left her oddly bereft, as though it were vital to her sense of well-being.

For a moment the disconnection aroused a tremulous uncertainty about what she was doing. Then Nick opened the door and his eyes blazed at her, seeming to dare her to step inside.

Her heart turned over. It was like the old days…was she brave enough to keep up with him, do what he did, share the thrills and the spills?

Pride and the long-held desire for his approval compelled her feet forward. Lights were switched on and the vista of his spacious living area diminished the sense of entering dangerous ground. The immediate impact was warmly inviting and she walked on without any prompt, eager to see his private world, to match it to the man who now wanted her in his life.

'This is lovely, Nick!' she cried, eyeing the two long sofas which dominated the lounge area, relieved and happy to feel real pleasure in his choices.

There was nothing intimidating here. The sofas were upholstered in a forest-green velvet with a tiny brown sprig pattern which lent more interest. Scatter cushions in gold and brown and green dressed the thickly rolled armrests, and beautiful gold lamps stood on side tables, giving a lovely mellow light.

A large square coffee table with a polished parquet surface provided easy service for anyone seated on either sofa, and floor-to-ceiling curtains beyond it obviously hid a magnificent view. As she tried to imagine it, Nick strode past her and operated the cord that pulled the curtains apart.

Even at night, the sheer scope of it was breathtaking, the lights of the city climbing upwards from the harbour shores, the island of Fort Denison floodlit, the moving lights of boats on the water.

'Oh!' she breathed in awed delight, instantly walking forward to see more. 'It must be marvellous to look out on this every day.'

'Yes. There's always something interesting happening on the harbour, liners coming in, yacht races, navy ships on the move.'

He was on the move, too, coming towards her, and his vibrant masculinity hit her anew, kicking her pulse into a faster beat. Suddenly he looked very aggressively male, the strong planes of his face gleaming more sharply in the lamplight, his eyes hooded, his body emanating deliberate purpose.

'I don't think you'll need this now,' he said, removing her wrap and dropping it on the end of the closest sofa.

His arm replaced it, curving around her shoulders and turning her as he gestured towards the dining area and the kitchen which had a bar separator from the rest of the living area and high stools where people could sit and converse with whomever was working behind it.

'The open plan allows the view to be enjoyed from everywhere,' he pointed out. The fingers stroking her upper arm stilled and tensed as he added, 'You get a similar outlook from the master bedroom. Come and see.'

She glanced up, sensing another underlying dare, a test of courage he would judge her on. His eyes briefly met hers, simmering with a challenge she didn't understand. Before she could sift it through her mind, he was propelling her along with him.

Hugged to his side, acutely conscious of his body heat and the muscular strength she was brushing against with each step they took, Barbie stopped seeing anything. She moved in a blur, the word, *bedroom*, pounding through her mind.

Wild fears and hopes leapt through her, causing nervous havoc. She didn't need to see the view again, but there was a terribly intimate attraction about being shown *his* bedroom, and somehow halting what was happening was not an option.

Another door was opened, lights switched on, and having swept her into this most private of all rooms,

Nick left her near the bed while he moved to the table on the other side of it and pressed a button on a console. The wall-length curtains on the far side of the room whooshed apart but Barbie was too distracted by the bed to look past it. She stood transfixed by the richly sensual temptation in front of her.

The top bedcover seemed to be made of softly glowing rows of sable fur, lushly inviting her to stroke it. Underneath was obviously a doona encased in stone-coloured raw silk. Piled against the bedhead were pillows in the same silk as well as of the dark brown fur, and even more stunning cushions in embroidered red velvet bordered by a leopard print.

'Is it real fur?' she asked, unable to stop herself from reaching out and running her hand over the thick, luxurious softness.

'No. Fake.'

'It feels real.'

'Yes, it does. A high-quality fake.' He walked back towards her, an ironic twist to his lips, his eyes glittering with a savage kind of mockery. 'It looks right. It feels right. Good enough to fool anyone that it's real. But it is an artificial simulation. Like you...'

'What?'

'...being a fairy princess. For children, you would seem very real, though in actuality you're a fake fantasy.'

She straightened up, jolted by the comparison, feeling as though her integrity was being attacked.

He rounded the bed, hands out, expressing an appeal. 'So I'm wondering...how real are you, Anne?'

Did he suspect some deception? How could he? Barbie struggled to collect her scattered wits. 'I don't know what you mean.'

He was close now, close enough to lift his hand and stroke her cheek, close enough for his eyes to burn into hers, seeking, demanding. 'You come to me in different guises, playing roles.'

'Just dress-ups,' she defended. 'I'm the same person underneath.'

He slid an arm around her waist and scooped her into full body contact with him. Her hands flew up, pressing against his upper chest, giving her some breathing space. She didn't understand what was going on here, only that she seemed to be on trial and Nick was fiercely resolved on not being fooled by her. Had his recent experience with Tanya scarred him?

'You *feel* right,' he said with a low throbbing vehemence that thrummed into her heart. His fingers slid into her hair, his thumb lightly fanning her temple as though wanting to infiltrate her secret thoughts. 'Do I feel right to you?'

Her body was quivering inside, whether from fear or excitement she didn't know. Her mind was a mess. The intensity of feeling pouring from him made any thinking difficult. She remembered how it had felt when he kissed her...no conflict then.

'Kiss me,' she whispered, the need to set everything right between them so urgent, she couldn't think further than that.

For a moment his eyes darkened with turbulent emotion. Panic increased Barbie's turmoil. It wasn't the answer he wanted. What was? What did he need from her?

Then his mouth crashed down on hers, hot and wild, and Barbie's panic surged into an equally heated response. It was not a kiss of sweet exploration, nor one of sensual pleasure. It was a passionate plundering, intent on smashing any barrier between them, a tempestuous testing of how far desire went, how *real* it was.

There was anger in it, frustration, the need to rip into each other, taking instead of giving, as though this was their one chance to get what had been missing from their lives and there was no other source for it. They were greedy for each other, feverish in their need to know, to prove the *rightness* they craved.

On some sane level Barbie knew she was being insanely reckless but didn't care. There was no turning back. Nick Armstrong was not in the lead now. She was not a little lamb following him. She was holding him to her and revelling in the feel of him, his hard maleness pressed against her, wanting entry to the woman she was, his mouth exploding into hers again and again, needing the essence of her, determined on having it.

His hand burrowed under her hair and scooped it off her back, hooking it over her shoulder, out of the way, as he found the head of her zipper and opened her dress. A leading advantage to him, she thought, and instantly dropped her hands to his shirt, tearing at the buttons. *I can do whatever you do,* was racing through her mind. *You won't leave me behind. Not this time.*

Clothes hit the floor. Shoes were kicked off. Strong hands almost encircled her waist, digging into her naked flesh, lifting her off her feet. She was tossed onto the bed, landing sprawled across the sable fur, sinking into its thick softness, the fibres caressing her bare skin with sinful sensuality.

And Nick stood there like a primitive caveman, his chest heaving, his eyes glittering over the prize he'd brought to his lair. 'You really want to go this far?' he demanded.

Echoes of the past rocketed around Barbie's mind, the doubt that little Baa-Baa Lamb could go the distance.

'I'm already this far,' she fiercely retorted and a woman-devil inside her drove her to stretch out provocatively. 'It's up to *you* to join *me*.'

He certainly had the superior strength. His magnificent body rippled with taut male muscles. But she had power, too, the power of being a woman he wanted, and his very evident erection made that undeniable. It was good he had to come to her. It was great to be the one he followed for once, had to follow because *he* needed to be with *her*.

She gloried in the sizzling flare in his eyes as he moved, one knee sinking into the fur beside her. He nudged her legs apart with his other knee, taking a subtle mastery over her position. A flood of vulnerability suddenly attacked her sense of power, but Barbie wouldn't let it win. She was not going to show

any fear to Nick. Even when he kneeled over her on
all fours, threateningly dominant, her eyes held his in
fierce challenge—no surrender in this game of games.

Come and get me, she silently dared.

No more hide-and-seek.

They were down to absolute basics, a man and a
woman coming together.

He took her mouth, invading it with such erotic
passion, her body instinctively arched for the more
intimate invasion. But he withheld it, resisting the pull
of her arms, tantalising her with the simulated promise of what was to come. She clawed his back. He
lifted his head. For a moment she saw the gleam of
savage satisfaction in his eyes, the triumphant knowledge of her frenzied need.

In the very next instant it meant nothing. He
moved, his head dipping down to her breasts, taking
their extended peaks in his mouth in turn, and all she
knew were the sweet bursts of pleasure he evoked
with the wild suction of his mouth, the exquisite lash-
ing of his tongue, pleasure she violently wanted pro-
longed, wanting more and more of the intense excitement he aroused. Her fingers raked through his hair,
grasped his head, intent on seizing control, moving
him to match her ravening need.

Again he eluded any submission to her will, tearing
himself out of her grasp, trailing his mouth over her
stomach, leaving kisses of pulsing heat, moving
lower, lower. A hand slid down the soft, moist folds
between her legs, fingers stroking, circling, caressing…mesmerising sensations. Her own hands stopped

scrabbling to hold him. The distraction was so intense she instinctively closed her eyes, her whole being drawn to concentrate on inner feelings.

Unbelievably, the enthralling touch was suddenly accompanied by a kiss so shockingly intimate she almost jerked away from it. An arm across her hips held her still and the shock melted away under the sweet flood of sensation his mouth wrought, delicious waves of it, peaking and spilling through her, gathering a rhythmic momentum that ultimately begged for a truly mutual mating.

'Stop!' The cry ripped from her throat, driven by a need she couldn't hold back, couldn't control, couldn't help herself. 'Come to me now, Nick! Now!'

She threshed against his hold, wild for him to do what he should. His arm lifted and burrowed under her. She reached for him, feverishly primed to fight for what she wanted. It wasn't right yet. It had to be right. But she didn't have to fight. He surged up and over her, making the entry she craved, the blissful joining, a deep penetration that filled her with rightness, a stunningly ecstatic rightness.

'Yes...' she breathed on a burst of relief, all her inner muscles squeezing him, hugging the wonderful pleasure of him.

'Open your eyes.'

A raw need gravelled through his command and Barbie instantly complied.

His eyes blazed into hers. 'Don't close them. I will not be a fantasy. This is very...' He pulled back, leaving her momentarily devastated by the loss of the deep connection. '…very real,' he harshly asserted, and drove forward, emphatically proving the power of his reality.

'Very real,' she agreed, exulting in the proof.

Slowly, tauntingly, he repeated the withdrawal, leaving her quivering in anticipation until he came again, filling the emptiness, taking possession of it, setting off convulsive ripples of intense excitement.

'It feels good?' His eyes glittered, demanding her admission, or was he mocking her need for him?

'Yes, yes…' she cried. 'You must know it does. Why are you asking?'

'Because I want to hear you say it.'

Was this about winning for him? Being on top?

'Don't play with me, Nick.' She lifted a hand to his face, urgently stroking an appeal. 'Just be with me. Don't you want that?'

He closed his eyes, expelled a long deep breath, and without another word, moved them both into an all-consuming rhythm, their bodies pulsing to the drumbeat of their union, a deep pounding of flesh within flesh that was totally exalting, primal, power- ful…fulfilling a long-dormant sense of destiny that had lain in Barbie's mind and heart for years and years and years.

Nick and her.

She loved the feel of him, loved the thought of him loving the feel of her. She didn't know how many times she climaxed around him. It was wonderful that he didn't stop, that he wanted to go on and on. She used her hands to transmit her sense of wonder and pleasure in him, caressing his beautiful body, adoring it, revelling in it, delighting in the excitement she stirred, the faster tempo of his driving into her.

It was only right that he should come to climax, too, the exquisite release of tension it brought, and she urged him towards it, using her whole body in a voluptuous tease, wanting to give him all he had given her.

And when he finally came, it was a magical sensation, the hot explosive injection of himself so deeply inside her, the intimate melding she could feel taking place, Nick relaxing, hugging her tightly to him, letting it be, the two of them joined as one...at peace.

What bliss to lie together like this! Even when he rolled onto his side, he carried her with him in close entanglement, and her head ended up resting over his thundering heart. Contentment seeped through her and she wished this lovely sense of well-being could go on forever.

Or was that a fantasy?

The thought brought back the memory of what Nick had implied earlier. She frowned, not liking what they were sharing linked to anything that wasn't real. Impulsively she spoke, wanting to clear any misconception he had about what she was doing here with him.

'This isn't a fantasy to me, Nick. More like a dream come true.'

The words filtered through his absorption in her glorious hair, the heady scent of it, the silky texture, the sensual pleasure of its soft flow over his skin.

What dream?

He frowned, remembering how she had continued to evade admitting who she really was, inviting him to kiss her, challenging him to take her, pleading for him to finish what he'd started. And the finishing had blown all the disturbing sense of wrongness out of his mind.

It was a struggle even now to focus on it when he felt so good with her. But she still wasn't telling him the truth about herself. He didn't want to think about the girl he'd turned away from him. He wanted to immerse himself in the pleasure of the woman in his arms, but he couldn't stop himself from wondering what dream Barbie Lamb might have nursed...a dream that had now come true.

Had she imagined taking him as her lover, showing him what he had missed all these years?

What was the next move?

Slapping him in the face with who she was, then leaving him with an unforgettable taste of what he could have had if he'd acted differently?

The buzz of torment in his mind was abruptly obliterated as her mouth closed over the nipple closest to his heart and she began licking and tugging at it. The unexpected burst of erotic tingling had his fingers winding tightly around her hair, pulling her head up. She looked at him, a joyful teasing dancing in her clear grey eyes.

'You did it to me, Nick. Now it's your turn.'

'Tit for tat?'

She grinned so openly, he couldn't believe she was taking him for a ride. 'Let me. I want to,' she replied, her voice a soft siren call that promised pleasure.

He let her.

Her kisses sent out streams of hot excitement and the delicate feathering of her fingers traced erotic paths all over him as she moved down his body, her soft female flesh pressing, sliding, arousing and inciting more sexual desire. Then her hands were cupping him, encircling him, stroking, lightly squeezing, making him swell with urgency.

He started to move, and she stopped him, laying an arm over his stomach as she took his re-erected length into her mouth and seduced him into stillness with the utterly exquisite sensations she delivered, not only internally, but externally with her long hair fanning his thighs and groin.

His muscles tensed. He knew he couldn't contain himself for long. She was taking him to the edge of control and suddenly he didn't want it this way. It was too one-sided. He jack-knifed forward, hauled her up and set her astride him, burying himself inside her to the hilt, loving her slick velvet heat.

'Ride me,' he invited, recklessly uncaring of any fall she had in mind for him.

She was a golden goddess, and she could steal his soul for all he cared at that moment. Her eyes sparkled with the power he gave her but she didn't flay him with it. She rode him slowly, savouring each long slide, and it was incredibly sexy, like a waltz designed to revel in secret intimacies. Like knowing her breasts were bare and accessible behind the veil of hair that had fallen forward over her shoulders, the thick silky tresses swaying, giving glimpses of dark areolae.

He reached under the veil, filling his hands with the lovely soft weight of them, feeling them move to the rhythm she chose, a secret pleasure, hidden from his vision but there in his hands. And any concern over where this night was leading was lost in the need, the compulsion to feel everything there was to feel with this woman.

It went beyond sexual gratification. The desire for more of her didn't stop at climax. Her body was endlessly exciting, her mouth a feast of sweet passion, her sense of sensuality more erotic than anything he'd known. She gave the much ill-used words, *making love,* real meaning, and it was that very loving which eventually soothed him into sleep, imbued with the feeling that nothing had ever felt so right.

It was a deep, peaceful slumber and nothing disturbed it. There was no sense of anything changing, no alarm signals slipping into his subconscious, no awareness of being left alone.

At six-thirty, the clock-radio beside his bed came on, signalling the beginning of another workday, music playing, bringing him awake. Barbie, too, he thought, not yet aware that she wasn't beside him.

With a smile already gathering from a flood of memories, Nick opened his eyes...and found she was gone from his bed, gone from his apartment...and there was nothing to say she would ever be with him again!

CHAPTER ELEVEN

NICK slid his Porsche into his parking slot behind the warehouse just as Leon was stepping out of his BMW. Bad timing. He wasn't in the mood for any personal chat with Leon and it was a dead certainty what the hot topic would be.

He switched off the engine and sat brooding over whether to get out or not. The urge to drive over to the Ryde apartment and confront Barbie Lamb face to face had been burning through him ever since he'd woken up and found her gone. It was still burning. But would such action achieve what he wanted?

If this was the fall she'd intended all along, nothing was going to change her mind, and he'd just be asking for more punishment. Alternatively, if she needed more time…time to think, to re-appraise, to decide she really did want him…time might be his friend. Either way, he hated the feeling this was Judgement Day.

Leon knocked on the window, mugging a comical query. Expelling a sigh of deep frustration, Nick opened the door, determined not to answer his friend's curiosity. He had no answers anyway, none that he liked.

'Well, did the beauteous Anne live up to your expectations?'

Nick glowered at him. 'Why don't you mind your own business, Leon?'

'I'm an interested party, remember?' came the quick retort.

Caught up in his own dilemma, Nick had forgotten about Leon's interest in Sue Olsen. He closed his door, locked the car, thinking Barbie's partner had to be well aware of the deception. And just where did that place Sue Olsen?

'She wasn't what you wanted after all?' Leon persisted.

'She's everything I want,' Nick declared, wanting an end to the inquisition. He needed more time to sort things out himself.

Leon glanced sceptically at him as they fell into step, heading indoors to their offices. 'So how come you're not bursting with happiness?'

'Because I'm not sure where she's at,' he shot back. 'Now drop it, Leon.'

'You didn't rush her, did you?'

'I said *drop it!*'

'Yeah. Right. Just so long as I don't cop any fallout from Sue.'

The feisty little redhead was in on Barbie's game. She had gone along with the Anne Shepherd cover-up yesterday. Maybe both women were taking him and Leon for a ride. Nick held his tongue, though he didn't care for the taste of these thoughts. No point in warning Leon until he knew what the play was. He certainly wouldn't be thanked for it.

'I hope you can give your full concentration to the interviews today,' Leon sliced at him.

'What interviews?'

Some under-the-breath muttering preceded a biting reminder. 'The ones where you decide on the two extra graphic artists you insisted you needed. Of course, I realise the pressures you're currently feeling have nothing to do with work, but...'

'Okay! I'll be ready for them. Roll them into my office when they arrive.'

'First one is ten o'clock.'

'Fine!'

'Take time to check their résumés again, Nick. We don't want misfits on the team.'

'I know how to look after my side of the business,' he snapped.

'Fine!' Leon snapped back and sheered off to his office, leaving Nick in no doubt about the friction he'd stirred.

He grimaced and carried on to his own office, boiling with resentment over being caught in this awkward situation. Why couldn't Barbie have been straight with him? And how in hell could she just walk away from what they had shared last night? Even on the most basic level, did she think that depth of sexual harmony could be found with anyone?

By the time he settled behind his desk, Nick knew he had to force a resolution, one way or another. It wasn't just himself affected here. Leon was involved, too. He picked up the phone book, found the number he needed, and jabbed the buttons on his telephone with grim determination. He heard the buzzing at the other end and fiercely willed it not to be followed by an answering machine.

'*Party Poppers,*' Sue Olsen's perky voice announced. 'How may we pop for you?'

Right out of the cake you and Barbie have baked, Nick thought, hellbent on having the sweet icing of deception burst asunder. It was on the tip of his tongue to ask for Barbie Lamb, tempted to surprise some relevant reaction out of her friend and partner in crime, but he really wanted the admission to come from Barbie herself, and freely given, not forced out of her.

'Nick Armstrong here. May I speak to...Anne Shepherd, please?' The false name almost stuck in his craw.

'Anne,' Sue repeated, as though it tasted sour to her, too. 'Could you hold please? I'll just go and get her for you.'

'Thank you.'

No *Drop Dead Delivery* from Sue Olsen. If that was on the agenda, she intended Barbie to do it herself. It could be that she didn't like this deception any more than he did. If Sue was truly attracted to Leon, it was certainly a complication she wouldn't welcome, with Nick being Leon's partner. She might be pressing Barbie to tell the truth right now.

Nick geared himself to play the conversation carefully. If there was a chance of winning, he didn't want to blow it.

*   *   *

'Wake up, sleepyhead! Rise and shine!'

Sue's adamant command penetrated Barbie's peaceful slumber and jerked her head off the pillow. 'What's up?' she asked groggily.

'*You* should be,' came the terse reply from her friend who was propped against the doorjamb, eyeing Barbie's bleary confusion without the slightest trace of sympathy. 'It's almost nine o'clock and lover-boy is on the *Party Poppers* phone.'

'Lover-boy?'

'Nick Armstrong. Let's get the personal stuff out of the way before business hours begin. Okay?'

'Nick... on the phone...' Her heart started to flutter.

'Asking for Anne Shepherd so I take it you didn't 'fess up.'

Barbie flung off the bedclothes and scrambled to her feet, struggling to clear her woolly head. Nick may well want answers to why she had left without telling him. How could she say that in the end, she hadn't quite trusted him to keep wanting her? After all, he didn't know who she was, and leading her into his bedroom so soon after meeting...was that his habit with any woman he desired?

Once he'd gone to sleep, the *bed and breakfast* thing had started haunting her, leaving her very uncertain about what the night had meant to him. She couldn't stay, couldn't handle being faced with...less than she wanted from him.

'I can't imagine what you managed to talk about until three o'clock in the morning,' Sue drawled.

'Couldn't have been about Barbie Lamb. And I doubt any restaurant stays open to that hour, either.'

'Three?' Was it that late when she'd left Nick's apartment? She hadn't looked at clocks. Too much else jamming her mind.

'It was almost four when I heard you come in,' Sue dryly stated. 'Did he take you on to a nightclub?'

'He's waiting on the phone,' Barbie reminded her, cutting off the inquisition. 'And we agreed this was my business, Sue.'

'Right!' she mocked, stepping back from the bedroom doorway to let Barbie out to the living area. 'Go ahead. Make a mess of things.'

She winced, knowing she could look for no understanding or helpful advice from her friend. 'Thanks for waking me up.'

'I wish you would wake up,' Sue muttered darkly, swinging away to go into her own bedroom, respecting Barbie's right to privacy with this personal call, despite strongly disapproving the relationship as it stood. 'And don't forget we've got a gig at the line-dancing club tonight,' she tossed over her shoulder. 'So no making other plans.'

On a beeline for the telephone, Barbie raised a hand to indicate she'd heard. Her mind was feverishly playing through what to say to Nick. This call had to mean he wanted to continue the relationship with Anne Shepherd.

Or have more sex with her.

Had it been a terrible mistake to go to bed with him? The memory of her madness in wantonly goading him into it burned through her as she picked up the receiver. Swamped by a rush of self-consciousness, 'Hi!' was all she could manage.

'Hi to you, too,' Nick replied. Then after a pause she didn't know how to fill, he added, 'I missed you this morning.'

Her cheeks bloomed with heat. 'I thought it best I go,' she gabbled. 'I wasn't sure…I mean…I'd parked the car in the street and…and I couldn't remember how long that was legal for, once it was morning and the traffic started up…and I knew Sue would be expecting me home…and…'

'And you didn't want to wake me to say goodbye,' he helped her somewhat dryly.

She sighed, relieved he seemed to be accepting her explanation. It was impossible to go into the emotional conflict he stirred because much of it was related to a history that still made her feel extremely vulnerable where he was concerned. More so after abandoning herself so utterly to him in bed.

'I did wonder if last night was as special to you as it was to me,' he went on after another pause she didn't know how to fill.

'Yes. Very special,' she said feelingly, unable to help herself from admitting she had been a very willing partner in their intimacy, revelling in it as long as it lasted.

'So there's nothing…troubling you?'

About a thousand things, but none she could bring herself to speak of. 'I'm fine, Nick,' she assured him.

'I'm sorry I left without a word but...it was late...and...'

'Yes, I understand. It simply occurred to me that talking was...limited...after we...connected in other ways. If there's anything you want to say...any concern... I do want to be with you again. Very much.'

'I want that, too,' she rushed out, recklessly squashing the doubts about the path he was treading with her. Time would tell, she told herself. She needed more time.

'Then what about tonight?'

Sue's warning stopped an eager assent. 'I'm booked to work tonight, Nick. I'm free tomorrow evening if that suits you.'

'Fine! I'll pick you up from your place at seven.'

'Here?' Barbie frowned, imagining Sue in the background making smart cracks. 'I don't mind meeting you in the city.'

'Better not to have problems with your car. I'm happy to take you home whenever you want to go. All you have to do is tell me.'

'Oh!' Guilt squeezed her heart. It had been wrong to sneak off as she had, leaving him wondering how she felt the morning after. 'I'm sorry, Nick. I should have written you a note. Come Wednesday night, I'll be ready on the dot of seven.' *And be off before Sue could get a look in.* 'You've got the address?'

'Yes. From the phone book. What apartment number?'

'Four.'

'Thank you. I'll look forward to seeing you.'

'Me, too,' she said warmly, and was smiling as she heard the disconnection and lowered her own receiver.

Nick was not smiling. He'd just given her another chance to open up to him but the deception ride was still on and he still did not know if it was a vengeance trip or a trial run towards a judgement on him. Now he had to wait two more days for the next move.

Just how far did she want him to commit himself before the truth came out...or before she cut him off at the knees? Had that been an act on the phone—the embarrassed apology and the warm pleasure in hearing from him?

Nick shook his head, the only certainty slicing through the pummelling of doubts was that he couldn't bear to carry on with her in this false way. It was dishonest on both sides, with him hiding his knowledge and her pretending to be someone who'd never entered his life before.

It had to stop.

It would be impossible for him to act naturally towards her tomorrow night. He'd be grinding his teeth at her duplicity if she persisted with it, and she'd just indicated she intended to. Nevertheless, directly facing her with the fakery was tricky business.

It might make her feel a fool, realising she *had* been recognised. She might even hold last night's plunge into intimacy against him, regardless of how it had turned into something...incredibly good... totally unique in his experience. Surely in hers, too.

He didn't want that twisted into something bad.

Though he was so twisted up inside at the present moment, he had to find some resolution that would work positively and get him out of this mess.

What he needed was some outside intervention that would force her hand, make her reveal the motivation that was driving her decisions. Once he knew precisely what he was dealing with, he could win her around to trying a future together. He couldn't believe she had done what she'd done last night, without feeling genuine pleasure in him.

So what outside intervention could he bring into play?

Leon?

He instantly dismissed the idea of confiding *this* problem to his friend.

Sue Olsen knew, but she had no reason to help him.

His sister popped into his mind. He had intended asking her to help him find the fairy princess. If she booked *The Singing Sunflowers*... yes, Carole would certainly remember Barbie Lamb. The secret would have to come out, because Carole might blab to her brother and there'd be no evading the truth any longer.

Nick reached for the telephone again.

He didn't stop to question the wisdom of the plan evolving in his mind.

He wanted Barbie Lamb, not Anne Shepherd.

And he wanted her tomorrow night.

CHAPTER TWELVE

'I DON'T see any preschoolers whooping it up,' Barbie said, eyeing the beautifully landscaped grounds that were totally empty of children. 'Are you sure you've got the right address, Sue?'

'I double-checked. She's probably rounded them up and put them inside for *the big surprise*.'

Barbie wasn't convinced. The exclusive little cul-de-sac in the high-class suburb of Pymble reeked of expensive privacy, not the place for young families. 'It doesn't feel right. And with the call only coming in yesterday…such short notice. Maybe it's some black joke.'

'Who cares? The fee was paid upfront. We're here. We go in,' Sue declared, dismissing Barbie's doubts. She checked her watch. 'Ten fifty-seven. Three minutes to showtime. Let's get our hats and cuffs on.'

They were already wearing their green bodysuits and yellow petal skirts. Barbie reached over to the back seat of the car and collected the rest of their costumes.

'There's a woman coming out of the house now,' Sue informed her. 'Probably been watching for us to arrive. Better be quick, Barbie. It's bound to be Mrs. Huntley. Looks the right age to be the mother of tod-dlers.'

The brown cuffs with the flare of yellow petals were easy to shove on, but the hat was tricky, positioning it just right for the full sunflower to circle their faces. In her haste to get fully costumed, Barbie didn't even glance at the woman. She was only too relieved that no mistake had been made and the party call was genuine since they were expected by the home-owner.

Sue was out of the car first, ready to greet their client. Barbie hurried to line up with her, pausing to pick up the portable sound system which they needed for their act. The music for the action songs little children loved was all prerecorded, ready to play, and Sue had said the client had agreed to activate it on cue, no problem with having a power-point handy.

'Hi! So glad you're on time,' the mother was saying. 'I have the children packed into the family room downstairs with the other mothers looking after them. I wanted you to be a surprise for them.'

It must be a split-level house, Barbie thought, although that wasn't obvious from the street. The sloping block of land disguised it.

'Mrs. Huntley?' Sue prompted.

'Yes, I'm Carole Huntley. Stuart and Tina are my children.'

'I'm Sue Olsen and this is my partner...'

Barbie quickly swung around to join Sue and smile at the client.

'...Barbie Lamb.'

The smile froze on Barbie's face as recognition hit. Carole Huntley was Carole Armstrong—Nick's sister! She'd been stylish at eighteen. She was even more

stylish now, her thick black hair brilliantly cut in a
short bob and her boutique clothes perfectly co-
ordinated.

'Barbie Lamb?' Carole repeated incredulously.
'You're not…?' Her bright blue eyes stared search-
ingly at the face that was encircled by a sunflower.
'Yes, you are. Those eyes are unmistakable. Barbie
Lamb, after all these years…' She shook her head in
amazement. 'I was Carole Armstrong. Remember?
Two years ahead of you at school? Danny's and
Nick's sister?'

'Carole…' Barbie repeated numbly, her heart sinking like a stone.

'My goodness! It must be…nine years. The last
time I saw you was at Nick's twenty-first birthday.
You sang.' Her face beamed with pleasure in her recognition. 'And you've made a career of singing?'

'A career of sorts,' Barbie mumbled, barely able to
speak over the shock of being confronted by a mem-
ber of Nick's family, her identity made certain by
Sue's introduction.

'How fantastic!' Carole burbled on, delight and
avid curiosity in her eyes—the same vivid blue as
Nick's. She laughed, taking in the whole of Barbie's
appearance. 'I must say you make a beautiful sunflower.' Her gaze slid to Sue in sparkling pleasure.
'Both of you.'

'Thank you,' Sue quickly returned. 'Hope the children think so, too. If you'll show us the way…?'

'Yes, of course.' Carole flashed an apologetic
smile. 'No time for memory lane right now.' As she

turned to usher them down the path to the front door, she looked appealingly at Barbie. 'Perhaps afterwards you'll stay for coffee? I'd love to catch up on your news.'

'We…we have another gig this afternoon,' Barbie lied, desperate for any excuse to get away.

'Not a good idea anyway, Mrs. Huntley,' Sue chimed in. 'It would spoil the illusion for the children. Best that we come and go.'

'Oh! I guess so.' Carole looked disappointed.

'You didn't say whose birthday it was, Stuart's or Tina's,' Sue rattled on, taking the heat off Barbie.

'Neither. Stuart is three and a half and Tina's not quite two. Stuart broke his arm last Saturday and hasn't been able to go to play-school. I thought I'd throw him a party to cheer him up.'

Which explained the short notice, Barbie thought dazedly, still plunged into turmoil by the terrible co-incidence of coming face to face with two Armstrongs through the *Party Poppers* business, both within *a week* of each other. And this meeting with Nick's sister could very well blow her cover as Anne Shepherd. Carole was always the gossipy kind.

The discomforting blue gaze targeted Barbie again. 'The accident stopped us from going to Nick's thirtieth birthday party. Which reminds me…'

'These things happen,' Sue cut in sympathetically, waving to the front door. 'Now before we go in, and since the children are in the family room out of sight…perhaps the best idea is for you to take our music box, Mrs. Huntley, and go ahead of us, plugging it in all ready to play. That way we can really make a surprise entrance.'

Barbie was intensely grateful for the timely distraction. She offered the player to Carole who took it and looked down at the control panel as Sue explained what had to be done.

'Yes, fine,' she agreed. 'It's okay for you to wait in the foyer for a minute while I go ahead and switch on. They can't see you from there.'

Finally accepting the focus on business, she ushered them inside the house, leaving them to watch the direction she took to the family room—straight ahead, down the stairs, along a lower-level foyer and through an archway from which the noise of a lively party drifted.

'Get yourself together, Barbie,' Sue whispered warningly. 'I can't do this act by myself.'

She took a deep breath, needing the oxygen to clear her whirling head. 'Thanks for taking the flack off me, Sue.'

'You looked like a stunned mullet. Just forget her and concentrate on the toddlers. The show goes on.'

'I won't let you down.'

'You'd better not. If the fat's in the fire, it's of your own making and it's not fair to burn me, too. If you don't perform, I'll kick you.'

'I'm ready.'

'Then let's do it and get out of here.'

They did it. From the moment they showed their sunflower faces in the archway, a dozen or so under-fives were goggle-eyed, then enthralled by the act that followed, repeating phrases of the songs when urged to, following the simple dance steps, clapping in time with the sunflowers, and beaming joy in the wonder of it all.

With her energy fiercely channelled into connecting with the children, Barbie was barely aware of the mothers who sat watching. She couldn't risk a look at Carole for fear of being put off her stride, and the other women present were simply blurs in the background. However, they did come in useful, keeping the children from following them as she and Sue bowed out after forty minutes of highly concentrated entertainment.

Carole, of course, had to follow them, bringing their sound system with her. 'That was absolutely marvellous!' she enthused, once they were outside with the front door safely shutting the children in the house. 'My friends thought so, too.'

'Great!' Sue replied, whipping out a small bundle of business cards she'd tucked in her sleeve. 'Please pass these around. It's lovely to work from recommendations.'

As Carole took them, Sue deftly relieved her of their property. 'Thanks so much for your help with the music. Perfect timing. Why not go back to Stuart and Tina now? Enjoy their excitement. We'll see ourselves off.'

'Yes. Nice seeing you again, Carole,' Barbie quickly put in, desperately hoping Nick's sister would take the hint and let her escape reminiscences which were not welcome in any shape or form.

Unfortunately the dismissal didn't work. 'No, I'll walk up to the car with you. I understand you have to get on your way, but I've just been thinking, Barbie...'

Please don't!

Somehow she stretched her mouth into a polite smile as they started walking up the path, but she wished Carole Huntley onto another planet.

'It's Mum's fiftieth birthday this coming weekend,' she went on, 'and my husband and I are throwing a party for her on Saturday night. Danny's even flying home from San Diego for it. A big family and friends get-together. Like Nick's twenty-first. It would be lovely if you could come...'

The reminder of Nick's twenty-first set up an instant and violent recoil. Words spilled out before she could even begin to relate the invitation to her current situation with him.

'That's very kind of you, Carole, but I'm not free.'

'Oh! What a shame! It would have been a great surprise to have you sing "Happy Birthday" to Mum. She always said you had a beautiful voice.'

The sheer insensitivity of that comment had Barbie grinding her teeth. 'I get paid for doing that now, Carole,' she bit out.

Carole instantly looked stricken by her blunder. 'I didn't mean for you only to come for that. I'm sorry if it sounded...' She heaved a mortified sigh, her eyes begging forgiveness. 'Our families used to be close. I just thought it would be nice to...'

'Perhaps another time.'

'Barbie, I honestly wasn't asking for a…a professional freebie. I wanted your company. The whole family would, I'm sure. And there'd be other old friends from Wamberal for you to catch up with.'

It took a huge effort to stretch her mouth into another stiff smile but Barbie managed it as her hand reached for the handle to the passenger door of the car. 'Well, it sounds like your mother will have a wonderful fiftieth. I hope you all have a marvellous time together.'

Hearing Sue open the driver's door—the cue for a fast getaway—Barbie nodded a farewell. 'Thanks again for the invitation. I'm afraid we must go now.'

'Yes, we must,' Sue echoed across the hood of the car. 'And may I say, Mrs. Huntley, you're very lucky to have such beautiful children. They're a delight.'

Which was a better exit line than any Barbie had given. It held Carole silent while they got in the car. Sue gunned the engine, and they were off, but not quite away. They had to use the turning circle at the end of the cul-de-sac, which brought them back past Carole who hadn't moved.

She stood on the verge of the road, her hands interlacing worriedly, her face obviously troubled. Barbie lifted her hand in a last salute, wishing she hadn't taken such quick offence at the tactless invitation. It would make the next meeting with Nick's sister awkward…if there was a next meeting. One thing was certain. She couldn't spin out the Anne Shepherd cover much longer with Nick. If brother and sister were in contact over plans for celebrating their mother's fiftieth...

'I take it Nick hasn't asked you to this big family do?' Sue inquired sardonically.

'No. Not yet.'

'Didn't even mention it in all the hours of talking you had last night?'

The mocking emphasis on *talking* goaded her into a heated defence. 'Why should he? To all intents and purposes Nick has only just met me. He doesn't know I know his family.'

Sue slanted her a derisive look. 'He's been stringing you along, probably to get what he wants, and I'll bet you spent more time in bed with him than anywhere else.'

'That's my private business!' Barbie grated, her hands clenching at her friend's cynical attitude.

'Then at least get the blinkers off your eyes and see it right,' Sue sliced back at her in exasperation. 'By the end of your night with him, it wasn't Anne Shepherd Nick Armstrong had in his head or anywhere else. He knows who you are. Or suspects strongly enough to put it to the test. What do you think that gig with his sister was about?'

Thrown into confusion by Sue's certainty, Barbie lost the final line of logic thrown at her. 'I don't know what you mean.'

'The booking came in from Carole Huntley just an hour after you talked to Nick yesterday, still pretending to be Anne Shepherd. If you can't put two and two together, I can. Before today is out he'll have confirmation from his sister that Sue Olsen's partner *is* Barbie Lamb.'

'It could have been a coincidence,' Barbie cried, trying to hold back the sickening wave of humiliation stirred by Sue's interpretation of events.

'And pigs might fly.'

'Nick couldn't have told her,' Barbie argued frantically. 'Carole wasn't expecting me. It was your introduction that triggered recognition.'

'Unmistakable eyes,' Sue tossed at her. 'How long did Nick gaze into them over dinner, Barbie? And don't forget I did call you Barbie in his office before you suffered a rush of blood to the head and gave yourself a false identity. You think he's slow at putting two and two together?'

Her stomach started churning at the memory of his comment on her eyes...a vivid reminder of the girl he'd once known.

'Face it!' Sue bored on relentlessly. 'The game is well and truly up. He used his sister as a check on your real identity and she's probably on the phone to him right now, reporting the outcome. So, for pity's sake, don't make a fool of yourself by trying to continue this crazy deception when he turns up tonight!'

A fool of herself?

Sue didn't know the half of it.

Nick's probing questions, his comments on fakery...her own behaviour in asking him to kiss her, ripping his clothes off and...none of it bore thinking about in the light that he had known—or suspected—

she was the very same Barbie Lamb he had once put out of his life.

She wished she could curl up and die.

'You know, that party Carole Huntley was going on about could be the party Leon invited me to,' Sue muttered. 'It's this Saturday night.' She shot Barbie a worried look. 'What are you going to do?'

She shook her head in hopeless distress. 'I don't know, Sue.'

'Well, I don't suppose you want to hear *I told you so*. At least you've got the rest of the day to work it out.'

Barbie closed her eyes, feeling too sick to talk.

'I hope you can work it into something good,' Sue said in a softer voice.

The sweetest revenge, Barbie thought, was also the path to hell.

CHAPTER THIRTEEN

NICK held his impatience in check until two o'clock to call his sister, knowing the children would need time to wind down from the excitement of the party and settle into their afternoon nap. He didn't want Carole distracted. He needed to pick her brains of every impression she had of Barbie Lamb.

The buzz of the call-signal grated on his nerves as he waited and waited for it to be answered. Finally the receiver was picked up and a breathless Carole said, 'Hi!'

'It's Nick, here. Where were you?'

'Cleaning up downstairs.'

'How did the party go?'

'Oh, Nick! You'll never guess...'

'Guess what?' His skin prickled with anticipation. It had to have happened... Barbie forced into facing that the deception couldn't work any longer.

'The party went fine. It was a great idea. The children loved it. And your suggestion to call *Party Poppers* and hire an act was brilliant. *The Singing Sunflowers* had them entranced...'

Get to the main point, Nick silently urged.

'But when the two performers turned up... Nick, one of them was Barbie Lamb! Remember Barbie?

The girl Danny had a big crush on back in our school days?'

'Yes, I do.' *The cat was definitely out of the bag.*

'I was so surprised. I had no idea she'd made a career with her singing. And she is good at it, Nick. Terrific, really. I would have loved to have a chat with her but...' A deep sigh.

'But what?' Nick prompted, uneasy with Carole's sigh.

'I don't think it was a nice surprise for her...seeing me again, I mean.'

'Why do you think that?'

'Well, she didn't enter into any reminiscences with me. You know how people do when meeting again after a long gap and our families *had* been close. It was all strictly business, cutting off any personal stuff.'

Shock, Nick thought, understandable in the circumstances.

'Which I didn't mind,' Carole rattled on, 'because I could see they were all keyed up to give their performance. And they certainly delivered marvellous entertainment.'

'I'm glad to hear it,' he encouraged.

'Anyhow, I thought what fun it would be for Barbie to come to Mum's party...you know, sharing old times and new...and I really put my foot in it, Nick. It's quite upset me actually.'

A nasty feeling crawled down his spine. 'Want to tell me about it?'

'Well, first off she stated flatly that she wasn't free

to come. And I must say it was a late invitation, so fair enough. Though she didn't even pause to consider if she might drop in for a bit. Even late if she had some work commitment. But I didn't notice the lack of any interest then.'

Nick frowned. There should have been interest if Barbie was seriously interested in him. Maybe she was just thrown at the prospect of having to confess to him beforehand. And *he* hadn't mentioned his mother's fiftieth birthday when they'd been talking families. His mind had been on trying to draw her out.

Carole took a deep breath and continued. 'I was wishing she could come and I made the mistake of saying how lovely it would be if she could sing for Mum, like she did for you at your twenty-first.'

Nick barely stifled a groan. Talk about triggering a bad memory!

'She gave me a look… I tell you it could have killed me stone-dead, Nick…and said she was paid for doing that now. Like I was presuming on her professional life, using her…it was awful. I just shrivelled up inside.'

'That was…unfortunate…to say the least, Carole.'

'I tried to recover, explaining how I felt…that it was a friendly thing…and she was frigidly polite…but I was left feeling like the lowest worm, Nick. And I really would have liked to get to know her again.'

'Perhaps you'll get another chance.' Nick hoped.

Was the power of attraction strong enough to override the damage done?

'No,' Carole came back, answering him very decisively. 'She couldn't get away fast enough. It's kind of sad. We were all close once. I didn't mean to make her feel I was just using her...like her friendship wasn't of any value except for how well she can sing.'

Using her... No, Barbie couldn't think he'd been using her for sex. She'd asked for it. Wanted it. Had she been using him? *A dream come true...*

Nick shook his head, realising he was veering off his sister's line of thought. 'You might have hit a raw nerve, Carole,' he said. 'Like with doctors being asked for medical advice when it's supposed to be a social occasion.'

Another deep sigh. 'You may be right. I guess people do get exploited in the entertainment world. And who knows what her life has been like since the Lamb family left Wamberal? It's been a lot of years. Maybe for her there's no going back.'

'No, we can't really go back.' Can't change anything we've done, either, Nick thought grimly.

'I've never been...*wiped*...so completely...'

The nasty feeling increased. 'I'm sorry you felt that, Carole.'

He hadn't foreseen this outcome. He'd wanted Barbie to come clean with him. The confrontation with his sister was telling him that any future with Barbie Lamb would be hard won, if it wasn't a complete fantasy.

'My fault...being so tactless,' Carole said glumly.

'There may be more to it than that,' he soothed, only too sharply aware of his guilt in creating this situation.

'Like what? She just doesn't want us in her life?'

'Could be.'

'That kind of blanket rejection is awful, isn't it?'

'Yes.'

And he was right back to how deeply his actions had wounded Barbie Lamb nine years ago. Deliberate actions...*like her deliberate action of provocatively inviting him to join her on his own bed*. The sweetest revenge of all? Nick Armstrong finding her irresistible, wanting her...wanting her beyond any doubt...*was that the dream come true?*

Carole gave a skittish laugh. 'Not that you'd know much about rejection since you're such an eligible bachelor.'

Nick had a gut-wrenching feeling he was about to know. In spades!

'My life isn't all a bed of roses,' he said with black irony. *It was more a bed of thorns. Or barbed wire.*

'Things not going so well with Tanya?' Carole teased.

'That's finished.'

'Oh! Are you bringing someone new to Mum's party?'

'My love-life is somewhat up in the air at the moment. Not a subject for discussion.'

'Okay. Well, thanks for listening, Nick. And Stuart did stop feeling sorry for himself. No grumpiness at all. The entertainment was a wonderful suggestion.'

'I'm glad to hear it worked for him. Give him a hug from me. Tina, too. Must go now.'

'Thanks for calling. It was good, talking to you.'

Good...

Nothing was *good!*

Nick put down the receiver, fighting the sense that at seven o'clock tonight, the woman who could have been everything he wanted, would proceed to deliver her ultimate revenge—wiping him out of her life.

But could she?

Maybe she had meant to drop him after the absolute proof of his wanting her on Monday night, except their coming together had been so special, she'd been tempted by the promise of feeling more of it.

He had that to fight with.

And fight he would.

On every level.

It was time she started seeing straight. And tonight he'd set her straight. The past was past and she had to let it go. For her own sake, as well as his.

Revenge didn't lead anywhere!

Not anywhere good.

And Nick wanted *good.*

For both of them.

CHAPTER FOURTEEN

'I'M OUT of here!'

The terse announcement from Sue sliced through the dark maelstrom of Barbie's thoughts. She lifted her head from the pillow where it had been buried for some time and tried to focus on her friend. 'Where are you going?'

'To a movie. Anywhere.' Her eyes flicked over Barbie's dishevelled state. 'It's obvious you don't plan on going out with Nick, and I'm not sticking around to be hit by flack from the showdown. The Anne Shepherd thing was your idea, not mine.'

'I can't go out with him. Not with this between us.'

'He's coming here,' Sue tersely reminded her. 'What are you going to do? Shut the door in his face?'

'I don't know. I don't know what I'm going to do,' she cried in anguish.

'Well, Nick Armstrong didn't strike me as the kind of guy who accepted having doors shut in his face, so I'm out of here. It's almost a quarter to seven, Barbie. You'd better start shaping up.'

Having delivered this last admonition, Sue was on her way, leaving Barbie to conduct her *private business* strictly on her own.

A quarter of an hour to go...

Pride forced her off the bed to tidy up her appearance. She exchanged her crumpled clothes for freshly laundered jeans and a blue-and-white checked shirt which she deliberately left hanging loose instead of tucking it in. She didn't want to emphasise her curvy figure, didn't want to look the least bit sexy to Nick's eyes.

She brushed her hair but didn't apply any make-up. Barbie Lamb, *au naturel,* she thought mockingly, staring at her reflection in the mirror. Nick couldn't say she was coming to him in different guises and playing roles tonight. Nothing fake about a bare face.

The doorbell rang.

Her heart, which had been a dead weight all afternoon, leapt to painful life, catapulting around her chest. The unconscionable rat, who'd knowingly given her enough rope to hang herself with, had come for another bite of her, loaded with the certainty she was here for the taking.

He'd known, before he'd swept her into his bedroom, that she was Barbie Lamb. Nothing that had happened there had anything to do with Anne Shepherd—a woman he'd just met and strongly desired. The admissions he had ripped from her in the heat of intimacy had been cold-bloodedly calculated to give him the upper hand in any further encounter with him.

She'd wanted him.

She'd begged for him.

She'd made love to him.

Burning with these humiliating memories, Barbie forced her legs to carry her through the apartment to the door Nick Armstrong was standing behind. She didn't want to open it, but Sue was right. He wasn't going away. And she was bitterly curious to know how he would explain his behaviour this time around.

There was no younger brother Danny lurking in the wings, providing some excuse for playing his game how he'd chosen to play it. And why he'd brought his sister into it today made no sense at all. He hadn't needed Carole's confirmation of her identity. It had been a cruel ploy, like a cat playing with a mouse before he pounced. Just as he had on Monday night.

On a burst of seething anger at his duplicity, Barbie unlocked the door and pulled it open, determined on blasting Nick Armstrong's confidence in manipulating what *he* wanted. Her grey eyes were as hard and as lethal as silver bullets, but the bullets hit a totally unexpected shield before they reached their target.

Her wings!

He was holding out her fairy princess wings...and they were fully restored to their former glory...no trace of damage at all!

One look at Barbie was enough to tell Nick there would be no playing happy families tonight. Tension whipped through him at the obvious evidence that all the female tools for generating sexual attraction had been abandoned. No makeup. Not even a dash of lipstick. And her clothes were more suitable for housework or gardening than for greeting a man whose interest she wanted to keep.

Wipe-out was telegraphed to him loud and clear.

Which meant she had been stringing him along to deliver the hardest, punch-in-the-heart rejection she could.

Anger pumped into a fierce wave of aggression.

He didn't deserve this.

And he wouldn't stand for it.

'Open the door wider so I can bring these wings in for you,' he instructed, determined to catch her off guard long enough to get inside. 'Don't want them damaged again.'

Apparently stunned by seeing them fixed, she stepped aside and let him in. Nick carried them right through the small living area and propped them against the wall next to a hallway which obviously led to bedrooms. He was now in the heart of her private territory and he wasn't about to give up the ground he'd made.

Barbie closed the door automatically, standing against it as she watched the unbelievable proof that he had cared enough to actually follow through on his declared intention. But when had he had the time to mend the broken wings? She felt as confused as she had at seeing them in his office on Monday.

'How did you do it?' she demanded, still seized by a sense of disbelief.

He swung to her with an ironic little smile. 'I contacted a fancy dress costume-maker on Monday afternoon and passed everything over to her.'

Her confusion flattened out. 'Someone else did it.'

'I wanted them to be perfect again.'

'Cost no object,' she muttered, remembering Sue's cynical attitude towards his fixing the wings. 'I guess you've found that money smooths the way to anything you want.'

His chin lifted slightly, his eyes narrowing into slits at her unappreciative reception of his effort. 'I simply wanted to give you pleasure.'

'Take it, you mean,' Barbie snapped. 'A whole lot of secret pleasure in leading Barbie Lamb up the garden path and seeing how far she would go.'

His head jerked in surprise at that accusation.

The fury that had been forcibly stored up inside her all afternoon, broke its banks and spilled forth, her eyes blazing contempt for his trickery. 'Don't think you can fool me anymore, Nick. I know you know who I am. I can pinpoint precisely when you realised who I am. Your comment on my eyes over dinner...'

'So why didn't you come out with the truth then?' he shot back at her. 'Why lie in the first place, and why continue the lie, despite every opening I gave you to admit who you are? Seems to me I was the one being set up as the fool.'

She folded her arms protectively, armouring herself against any firepower he thought he had against her. 'I didn't want you to connect me to any memories you had of *Baa-Baa* Lamb.'

'I never called you that, Barbie.'

'You thought it of me, always following you around whenever I was given the chance. So much so I caused a problem for you and you had to put a stop to it.'

His mouth thinned, biting back any further denial.

'Anne Shepherd let me be *me now*,' she cried, hating the knowledge he'd hidden to pursue his own way with her. 'It let me meet you without you thinking of me like that. *Me now*, Nick, and when it stopped being *me now*, you should have told me. Instead of which you chose to play your own secret game.'

'It was *your* game,' he retorted, anger blazing into his eyes. 'And I didn't know what the hell you were up to.'

'If it worried you, why didn't you come straight out with it?

'And have you walk away from me?'

'As you did from me? Bit of guilt there, Nick? Did you decide I was out to get you and dump you?'

Heat speared across his cheeks. 'It was a possibility,' he answered tersely.

'So instead of risking that possibility, you set out to colour the past differently, spinning me that story about Danny, making yourself out to be the noble older brother, standing aside for him to step in.'

'It was the truth,' he asserted emphatically.

She tossed her head in scorn for his truth. 'Well, you certainly weren't standing aside for anything this time. It was straight up to your apartment, into your bedroom…'

'You could have stopped it anytime,' he sliced in, the air between them sizzling with a ferment of cross-currents.

'So could you,' she hurled back, and out poured the tumult of bitter feelings his deception had stirred.

'You were getting too much of a kick out of it, weren't you? Remembering I'd once had a crush on you, and here I was, all grown up enough to whisk off to bed. Did it feel great, getting me to admit I wanted you, driving me to the brink, then holding off to make me beg for you...'

'Damn it!' he exploded, his hands whipping up in an emphatic gesture of frustration. 'You're twisting everything around. I just wanted you to admit who you were. I wanted it to be real between us.'

'How much more flesh-and-blood *real* can you get?'

'I didn't think you'd go that far and when you did, still without identifying yourself—and I gave you every chance to, Barbie—' He started walking towards her, his hands spreading in appeal.

'You stop right there, Nick Armstrong!' she commanded, her eyes flaring a fierce warning. 'I'm calling the shots now!'

He stopped, his hands falling to his sides, clenching. 'You were calling them all along, Barbie. The fairy princess act you played was designed to stir me up, and don't you deny it.'

'Yes.' Her chin went up in belligerent pride. 'I wanted to get a different reaction from you than I got at your twenty-first birthday party.'

'A sweet slice of revenge.' He nodded as though he'd known it all along, his eyes glinting accusingly as he read more into it. 'Did it give you a kick, doing the walking away after you'd sung to me this time around?'

Barbie refused to feel guilty. He'd made her pay for what little vengeance she'd taken on him. 'That was the intention,' she frankly acknowledged. 'But when you kissed me...' The memory of her response caused a rush of hot blood to her cheeks. '...it stirred everything up for me and I wished I hadn't done it.'

'Until you had second thoughts and came to my office to see if there was more *reaction* to be had,' he bit out grimly. 'And when there was, you carried it further...and further...taking me where you *wanted* it to go. And don't you deny that, either.'

'I didn't know you had Barbie Lamb in your mind,' she flung back at him in a fury of resentment.

'But you had *me* in *your* mind.' He started walking towards her, seething with the accusations he continued to hurl. '*You* were remembering. All the time you were remembering. Questioning me. Putting me on trial. Do you think I didn't feel it?'

'I didn't mean you to feel it,' she countered, although what he said was true, making her feel uneasy about her own private agenda and prompting a defence. 'I just wanted to find out where I stood with you.'

'Without letting me know where I stood with you,' he mocked. 'And just how long was that to go on for, Barbie? When was Anne Shepherd going to turn into you? When you'd had enough of me so you could do what you meant to do in the first place? Leave me wanting you and walk away?'

'I wasn't out for revenge. Not after the fairy princess thing. I just wanted to be sure I wasn't some fly-by-night affair to you before I laid myself on the line. I would have told you once I felt safe with you,' she defended, drawing herself up tautly, unfolding her arms, ready to fight as he closed in on her.

He came to a halt directly in front of her, using the power of his physique to make her feel she was on the judgement stand. His eyes glittered a savage challenge as he continued his cross-examination.

'So why treat my sister as you did…if you really wanted some future with me? You rejected her attempt at reviving an old friendship and her invitation to a family celebration.'

'I was in shock. The coincidence…except it wasn't a coincidence,' she threw at him bitterly. 'You shouldn't have dragged your sister into it.'

'It was the only way I could think of to make you stop hiding from me. And to flush the truth out of you. I needed to know what was in your heart…hope for some future with me or vengeance for what you obviously perceived as my rejection of you.'

It had been hope. But it was painfully obvious there was no hope of any understanding between them now. The situation was irreparably damaged by her deception and his reaction to it, making it impossible to see where the truth lay anymore.

His eyes raked derisively over her clothes. 'Seeing you dressed like this, the answer is clear. You're even standing by the door to show me out.'

Was this the end of what had started so promisingly on Monday night? Was this the end she wanted? Her sinking heart screamed no. Her mind scrambled to find some saving grace. Before she could say or do anything he moved. His hands fell on her shoulders, curling around them as though he was going to shake her.

'But not quite yet, Barbie. Before I leave…I'll give you the sweetest revenge of all.'

His face was so close to hers, his eyes were like magnets, drawing on her soul. Her mind was torn, wanting to deny she'd ever set out to be vengeful, yet guiltily aware that she had secretly revelled in scoring off him.

His grasp loosened and his hands slid along her shoulders, up her throat, cupping her face as he spoke with an intensity that gripped her heart and squeezed it. 'I want you, Barbie Lamb. Even knowing you're intent on twisting the knife and turning me out of your life, I still want you.'

His fingers stroked slowly up her cheeks, into her hair above her ears, raking it behind her lobes. 'Is that sweet to hear?' His eyes burned into hers. 'Let me make it even sweeter for you. Much better to taste the wanting, feel the wanting.'

Her heart was pounding so hard she couldn't think. Couldn't move, either. His head was bending and she knew he was going to kiss her. The sizzle of challenge was in his eyes, heating her blood, stirring needs she couldn't repress, memories of how it had been together.

Then his mouth was covering hers, his warm lips grazing seductively, igniting tingles of excitement, his tongue tantalising, not forcing an opening but holding out the tempting promise of deeply plummeting passion surging between them.

Would it happen again? Even now? With so much negative turmoil still churning away inside her? Helplessly distracted, Barbie couldn't resolve what was right and wrong. And her mouth craved a deeper kiss, a more telling kiss. No conscious decision was made. Her lips parted of their own accord and let Nick Armstrong in.

Instantly sensation swamped her. From the top of her scalp to the extremities of her toes every nerve came alive with excitement and the anticipation of more excitement. His kiss was so powerfully invasive, so passionately penetrating, resisting it was utterly impossible. Any such thought didn't even enter her mind. There was no thought, only a wild surge of need to possess him just as pervasively. It triggered a fierce response.

Her hands flew around his head, fingers clawing through his hair, holding him to her. He dropped his arms, wrapped them around her back and hauled her body into hard-pressed contact with his. There could be no mistaking his arousal, his desire for her. The wanting was not a lie. She *could* taste it, feel it, and again Barbie revelled in it, exulting in his taut masculinity, every bit of him straining to satisfy his need to capture and possess the whole sense of her.

She felt his hand move under her shirt, sliding up her bare back, unclipping her bra, and the instant loosening of her clothing shot a spear of alertness through the haze of her own urgent wanting. Was this right…this mind-blowing drive for sexual release?

Her breasts were aching for his touch. She was acutely aware of his hand gliding under her arm, reaching the soft swell of her flesh, nudging aside the unfastened bra, fingers encircling, softly squeezing, thumb fanning her nipple which was so hard and sensitised, the shock of pleasure had her moaning for more. She didn't want to stop it, didn't want to pause to consider anything.

Until he stopped it, dropping his hand to the waistband of her jeans, seeking to pull open the stud fastening. The realisation that he meant to take her right here, up against the door, shook Barbie out of her complicity in the intimacies that were fast leading to absolute commitment to the desire raging through her. Was this the only level of *wanting* Nick felt for her? Was he using sex in a last drive to keep her with him…for more sex?

The sudden pain in her heart eclipsed the needs pounding through the rest of her body. Her hands shot from his hair and slammed against his shoulders as she wrenched her mouth from the passionate persuasion of his.

'No!' It was a raw gasp. She threw back her head, gulping in more air. 'No!' It was an anguished cry, vehemently denying the physical upheaval pleading against this enforced parting.

'This is the you now, Barbie. The me now. You feel it. I feel it. Give it a chance,' Nick pleaded hoarsely, his eyes blazing conviction.

His arms wrapped around her again, hands curling around her buttocks, lifting her into an intimate fit with his erection, blatantly reminding her of what they had shared before. 'What we have together is very special,' he declared, his voice throbbing in her ears. 'You know it is. And I won't let you walk away from it, just because I did what I thought was best for you nine years ago.'

Best for her!

The cruellest cut of all…without so much as a word of kindness to soften it?

He was lying!

The wanting now was no lie, but he was trying to manipulate her feelings, just as he had manipulated them on Monday night. Today, as well, arranging the confrontation with his sister. This was Nick wanting his own way, getting his own way, never mind what she felt. Just like nine years ago.

She slammed her hands against his chest and pushed with all her strength. 'Let me go! Get away from me!'

The violence of feeling in her voice and action effected separation from him. He stepped back, releasing her and lifting his hands in vehement appeal, his face expressing angry bewilderment at her rejection. 'Why?' he demanded. 'You were with me. Just as you were when we made love on Monday night. I wasn't forcing myself on you.'

'No. But sex doesn't override everything else. Not for me it doesn't,' she cried, her eyes accusing him of taking unfair advantage of her vulnerability.

'It's been the most honest thing between us,' he claimed, and counter-accusation simmered through every word.

'You've got that right. But I want more honesty than straight-out lust. *Best for me,*' she mocked. 'All you've ever cared about is what was *best for you.* You didn't care about my feelings nine years ago and you haven't cared about them now...trapping me with your sister...not allowing anything to run any way but yours.'

His face tightened as though she had physically slapped him. He shook his head. When he met her gaze again, his eyes were bleak, no longer fired up to fight her. 'I did think it was best for you, Barbie,' he said quietly. 'You were a very special person. Too special to let your life be so singularly focused on me. At sixteen, there was so much more for you to discover, to explore.'

His calm reasoning flicked raw wounds. It felt as though he was the wisely objective adult explaining something to a child and she was no longer a child. She hadn't been a child for many, many years. Stung unbearably by this lack of emotional involvement with her, she picked a flaw in his condescending logic and lashed him with it.

'If I was so special, why didn't you ever look me up, Nick? After I'd had time to discover what you thought I should discover.'

It didn't sting him. He shrugged. 'Life happens. You moved away. I got involved with business.'

The flat statements goaded her further. 'The truth is you never gave me another moment's thought until I entered your life again.'

'No, that's not true.' He dragged in a deep breath and grimaced as he sighed. 'I can't change the past. I am sorry you were so hurt by my decision. I know I didn't handle it well.'

The old devastation of that night came flooding

back…the need to show him, to see appreciation and understanding in his eyes. Only it wasn't there. He'd decided it couldn't be. She searched his eyes now, wanting evidence of feeling for her, some caring warmth, even the heat of desire. There was not so much as a spark in them…dull, lifeless, defeated.

'After that…' he went on, his voice softer, a sadness in it that galvanised her attention, freezing her resentments. 'Well, I thought your life would have grown a long way away from me. And it has. Too far for me to reach you. I wish it were different…but there is no second chance.'

He reached into his shirt pocket and brought something out, his gaze dropping to it as he turned it over in his hand. A watch! An old watch! Barbie's heart lurched as recognition hit her. Surely she was mistaken. It couldn't be the watch she'd given him…

'Take it,' he commanded gruffly.

She did, in a daze of disbelief, turning it over to see. There on the back was the tiny lamb she'd had etched on it—the silent promise to follow him anywhere. He had kept it all these years…

'I may not have looked for you, Barbie, but I never forgot you.'

Before she could even lift her head, or think of a word to say, he stepped around her, opened the door, and walked out of her life.

CHAPTER FIFTEEN

ONE more chance…

Barbie willed it to be so as she carefully sprayed the silver glitter over the long gleaming waves of her hair. It was important to get her appearance absolutely right…as well as everything else. The fairy princess had to work real magic tonight. This was going to be the most critical performance of her whole life. Any possible future with Nick hung on it.

Surely he would realise it was hope driving her, not vengeance. Yet as she put the spray can down on her dressing-table and her gaze fell once more on the gift watch he'd returned to her, fear gripped her stomach. Had she killed hope…rejecting his explanations, rejecting his inner angst over her motives, rejecting the sexual attraction between them, rejecting everything he was?

She picked up the watch and rubbed her thumb over the etching of the tiny lamb for luck. She had meant what it had once promised—to follow him anywhere. If only she had carried that through this time—trusting instead of judging so badly—the terrible outcome with Nick might have been avoided. Following him tonight had to work. *Had* to.

She slipped the watch into her handbag. Nick had kept it for nine years. He hadn't thrown it away.

Maybe it would act as a good-luck charm, not letting Nick throw her away tonight.

Her mirror reflection told her she was as ready as she was ever going to be. If she made a total fool of herself, it didn't matter. It was impossible to lose more than she had lost, and if she won... Her heart quivered at the thought of having Nick look at her again as though she was the most desirable woman in the world to him.

She took a deep breath and set off on the journey that would settle her future with him one way or another. Leon Webster had picked up Sue two hours ago so the party for Nick's mother should be in full swing by now. Her appearance would be as much a surprise to them as it would be to everyone else, and Barbie could only hope Sue would understand.

Confiding in her friend might have triggered quarrelsome discussions and to Barbie's mind, there was nothing to discuss. Only this action could give her another chance with Nick. And she had the excuse that Carole Huntley had asked her to come and sing. If Nick didn't respond...well, she could leave straight afterwards and the performance should have no bearing on Sue's involvement with Leon.

The mended fairy wings and magic wand had already been carefully placed in the car, along with the music she needed. Barbie double-checked she had everything before settling herself in the driver's seat. From Ryde to Pymble was a relatively easy trip, yet it seemed nerve-rackingly long to Barbie, having to concentrate on traffic lights and being in the right lanes for turns.

When she finally reached her destination it was to find the cul-de-sac crowded with parked cars. To her deep relief, there was enough space left on the Huntleys' driveway to get her car off the road and close to the house. It blocked other cars from leaving but that was of no concern right now.

She fumbled with the fairy wings, fumbled with the wand, fumbled with the tape recorder. It was a major effort getting the necessary items out of the car without dropping them, even more difficult to position the wings to slide into their slot on the back of her dress. She wished she had Sue to help her, but even now she felt it was wrong to involve her friend in what was—as Sue said—her private business.

Having settled the wings properly, and fiercely focusing her mind on carrying through what she'd determined to do, Barbie managed the walk down the front path without mishap. The party noise seemed to be emanating mainly from the back of the house, which, she told herself, would make her entrance easier. Silently reciting her set speech about being a hired professional act, she rang the doorbell and hoped whoever answered the summons would accept her explanation without question.

What if it was Nick?

Her heart stopped with the shock of that thought. Dizziness clouded her mind. She stood in a state of total paralysis until the door opened and she was faced with a blessed miracle.

Carole Huntley.

'Barbie...?' she queried in astonishment.

Words rattled out. 'I've come to sing for your mother. You asked me... I can fit it in after all and I thought...you said it would be something special for her...'

'Oh! What a lovely surprise!' Carole instantly enthused. 'I'm so glad you could make it. And coming from some other professional engagement...' Her eyes were busily taking in the fairy princess costume. 'You look wonderful, Barbie.'

'It's all right then...'

'Fantastic!'

'Will you put the music on for me, Carole?' She held out the tape recorder. 'All you need do is press Play.'

'Of course.'

'Are they all downstairs?'

Carole's vivid blue eyes sparkled with conspiratorial pleasure. 'Wait here a minute and I'll herd everyone into the family room. Where Stuart's party was, remember? We can make it the same kind of surprise you gave the children.'

Relief poured through Barbie. 'That would be perfect, Carole.'

An anxious frown suddenly appeared. 'I'll pay you for this, Barbie. I never meant to...'

'No. Please...let's just do it. If you leave this door open a bit so I can come in when I hear the music...'

Carole hesitated a moment. 'Well, we can talk about it afterwards. Can you stay?'

'Yes,' Barbie said with a hope and a prayer.

'I'm so glad!' Her smile was all delight. 'Five minutes maximum to get everyone in place and quieten them down. Just slip in and close the door behind you when the coast is clear and you can be at the head of the staircase ready to make your entrance when the music starts. Okay?'

'Fine! Thanks Carole. There'll be two songs and "Happy Birthday" is second, so don't think you've got the wrong tape.'

'This is fabulous, Barbie. Mum's going to love it.' Excitement beamed from a wide grin. 'I'm off to set the scene.'

Luck *was* with her, Barbie feverishly assured herself as she waited, hearing Carole ordering around everyone inside, footsteps obeying her bidding, heading downstairs, the party noise lowering to a mood of expectancy. She peered around the door, and seeing the coast was clear, carefully manouevred herself into the foyer. Her fingers gripped the fairy wand hard as she wished for more luck, all the luck in the world.

It was quiet below.

She stepped to the head of the staircase and willed her legs not to start trembling on the way down. She swallowed hard to moisten her throat. The music started, providing the right backing for her voice. She took a deep breath. This was it! No retreat. The cue came...and she sang, pouring all the hope and longing from her heart and soul into the words...

'''*Somewhere over the rainbow...*'''

Never had her voice been so true, so powerful...but

Barbie didn't know it. She sang because she had to, and she walked down the stairs with all the majestic dignity of a fairy queen on the mission of a lifetime, not hearing the mutterings of surprise and appreciation, nor the hush settling as she descended to where the party guests were gathered.

Carole had obviously ordered them to circle the family room and those standing across the open entrance to it shifted aside to give Barbie a clear passage. Furniture had been moved back against the walls, probably to leave plenty of space for dancing. The centre of the room was completely empty.

As Barbie glided past the circled guests, she saw Nick's parents, Judy and Keith Armstrong, seated in armchairs at the far end. Beside them stood their family, Nick and a grown-up Danny near their mother, Carole and presumably her husband next to their father. All of them—except Nick—were smiling broadly, enjoying *the surprise*.

Barbie did her utmost to block his grim look out of her mind as she proceeded to the centre of the room, though she was conscious of her heart skipping into a faster beat. She couldn't let fear unfocus her. The song had to be sung without falter. She caught sight of Sue, and it was some relief to see her friend nodding approval and giving a thumbs-up sign.

Would Nick accept that after the most dreadful, damaging rain, a rainbow *could* appear, and he was the dream she was chasing tonight?

Barbie's whole being pleaded for that outcome as she halted and faced his mother to deliver the last poignant lines of the song, starting with the fantasy promised in the word—'"If..."' pouring faith and hope and optimism through her voice, needing to reach him, offering the chance—another chance—*if* he wanted to take it. She spread out her arms in a gesture of giving, willing him to understand, and the last line was a cry to him, if only his heart was open enough to hear it.

Loud applause erupted after the final note faded into silence. Judy Armstrong's face was crumpled with emotion, smiling through tears. Keith passed her a handkerchief, nodding benevolently at Barbie. She smiled back at both of them and risked a quick glance at Nick. He was not smiling, but his head was cocked to one side, his eyes narrowed on her, and his expression had subtly changed to a weighing look.

Barbie's heart skittered with wild hope. She wasn't facing a steely wall of resistance. He was receptive. At least a little bit.

Carole called for quiet, waving her arms to warn there was more. The introductory chord for the next song broke over the hub-bub, bringing a quick silence. It was not the sexy musical treatment Barbie had requested for Nick, more the sentimental traditional version of 'Happy Birthday,' and she gave it a lot of warm heart as she sang it to his mother, moving slowly forward, lifting the wand to release a sprinkling of magic glitter as she completed the song.

'Make a wish,' she softly urged as she bent to kiss Judy Armstrong's cheek and murmur her own personal, 'A very happy fiftieth birthday.'

'Thank you, Barbie,' she replied huskily. 'You've just made it extra special.'

'It's our song, *Over the Rainbow,*' Keith said gruffly. 'You sang it better than Judy Garland, Barbie. Wonderful to have you here.'

'My pleasure,' she mumbled, touched by his pleasure.

'Carole...' Keith turned and signalled his daughter. 'Play that music again. Your mother and I are going to dance to it.'

'Okay if I rewind the tape and play it again, Barbie?' Carole asked eagerly.

'Go right ahead.'

Stepping aside to allow room for Keith and Judy to rise from their chairs and take the floor, Barbie found herself lined up next to Danny who instantly caught her free left hand and squeezed it, drawing her startled attention to him. There was nothing shy in his face now. He grinned at her, his eyes sparkling the open appreciation of a mature young man who was very confident with women.

'Great singing!' he complimented, not the slightest trace of his old stutter marring his speech. 'Great homecoming for me, too, meeting you again, Barbie. You sure have grown into a stunner.'

And very desirable...

But it was the wrong man telegraphing that to her. She had never been interested in Danny. She wasn't now. Her gaze darted anxiously to Nick. Did he care that his brother was claiming her like this?

He was watching her, his eyes burning with questions that seared her soul. *Why are you here? What do you want? How much is real? Is it hope or vengeance?*

The music started again.

'How about dancing with me, Barbie?' Danny asked.

'No!' It was a hard, vehement negative.

Danny's head jerked in surprise to his older brother.

Nick glared at him, his whole body tense, emitting a fierce aggression. 'Not this time, Danny. Barbie is not yours to have. She never was. And I'm claiming this dance. Just step aside and go find yourself another woman.'

Danny gaped at him, stunned by the violent feeling he'd stirred in his older brother. He released Barbie's hand to raise both of his in an appeasing gesture. 'Hey, man! Take it easy! I was only...'

'Butting in, as you did nine years ago, wanting all Barbie's attention.'

'Hell!' His face flushed at the memory. 'That's ancient history, Nick!'

'Not to me it isn't,' came the savage reply. 'Back off, Danny. Now!'

'Okay! Deck's clear. Your play,' Danny babbled as he backed off, still wide-eyed and red-faced at his older brother's hostile reaction.

Nick stepped forward and scooped Barbie into a dance hold, his eyes blazing into hers, commanding acquiescence. Her heart catapulted around her chest as the arm encircling her waist pulled her closer, very firmly possessive in its strength of purpose.

'Hold it right there, you two!' Sue's voice whipped in. 'I'll take that.' She snatched the wand out of Barbie's hand. 'Leon…' She passed it to him. '…I've got to remove the wings and hook up the train of her dress so nothing gets torn.' Which she proceeded to do at lightning speed, Leon standing by to be handed the wings as well as the wand for safe-keeping.

'Sue's right. No more damage,' Leon admonished them.

'You can dance now,' she granted them. 'Or fight. Or carry on like lunatics if you must.'

'Are you quite finished?' Nick growled, the tension flowing from him wrapping around Barbie and holding her still and silent, everything within her tautly aching for positive responses from him.

'Quite!' Sue assured him. 'Leon, now that we've rescued the fairy princess costume, let's get out of the danger zone.'

'I'm with *you*, babe!'

Off they sailed in happy harmony with each other—twin souls who knew how to order *their* world, leaving Barbie and Nick to sort out whatever needed sorting in their very private business.

Her hand now freed of the wand, Nick took it, interlacing his fingers with hers to seal his grip. 'Tell me this is no game, Barbie,' he demanded, the intensity of his gaze brooking no attempt at deception.

'It's no game, I promise you,' she answered fervently.

His parents twirled past. 'Are you two dancing or what?' his mother asked in amusement.

Rather than draw more curious and interfering attention, Nick pushed his feet into dancing, gathering Barbie closer as he moved her to the slow beat of the song. She was acutely conscious of his thighs brushing hers, her breasts pressing against the warm wall of his chest. Her heart seemed to be thumping in her ears. She barely heard the music.

He bent his head beside hers and she heard the words he spoke, although they were barely above a soft murmur. 'Are you holding out a new start for us?'

Did he want it?

Panic seized Barbie. She had to give him the right opening, make this chance different to the last one.

'I did it all wrong, using a false name. I know I did. And I'm sorry I messed everything up between us,' she pleaded anxiously. 'My only excuse is...as Barbie Lamb, I felt so...so vulnerable, Nick.'

His chest rose and fell and she felt his sigh waft warmly through her hair. Then came the low, regretful words— 'I moved too fast. I cursed myself for it afterwards. If I'd let you go on as Anne Shepherd, you might have learnt to trust me.'

He was thinking back, not forward. She didn't hear hope in his voice, only sadness for mistakes made, and Barbie felt a dark weight descending on her heart. He didn't believe they could recover what had been lost.

The music stopped.

Nick released her from his embrace, and for one terrible moment, Barbie felt the most devastating despair. It was over. There was no chance. Then he grasped her hand again and into her shattered mind swam his command, 'Come with me!'

He pulled her with him, weaving past the party guests who were now responding to the second music track, loudly singing 'Happy Birthday' to Nick's mother. He slid open a glass door which led onto a patio and drew her outside, quickly shutting the door behind them. They walked to the end of the patio, around a corner of the house, into a pool of darkness.

'We should be private here,' he muttered, dropping her hand and moving away a few paces, establishing distance between them before turning to face her.

Barbie was beyond knowing what his actions meant. A fragile hope whispered he was still with her, though standing apart. He wanted to talk, if nothing else, and talking might help. But her mind was incapable of producing anything to say.

'The issue was always one of trust, wasn't it?' he declared, shaking his head as though in torment. 'I broke it so badly nine years ago...'

'Let's not revisit that time, Nick,' she begged, craving only a future with him.

'I have to make you understand, Barbie. We can't paper over this,' he said vehemently. 'I need you to know you *were* special to me. Even when you were just a little girl, you had this way of looking at me...your eyes so full of innocent trust...like you believed nothing bad could happen to you because I was there to look after you.'

'It's called hero-worship, Nick,' she said derisively, wanting to stop him from looking back, frightened that it couldn't lead anywhere good.

'No, it was more. No one else ever gave me that sense of…a pure love. It made me want to live up to it. I guess you could say I fed on it, Barbie, until I came to realise how selfish that was. I convinced myself I was giving you something—a broader life—when I forced the break. But what I broke was your trust in me.'

It was *true love,* Barbie wanted to cry, but she bit her lips, not brave enough to speak that truth.

'I hated having done it, having lost it,' he went on. 'And I knew it could never be recaptured. So when I recognised Barbie Lamb in Anne Shepherd…it hit me hard, the knowledge of breaking your trust. I wanted you to give it to me again, and when you didn't, I began not to trust you instead of facing up to what I'd done and the repercussions of it.'

He spread his hands in an urgent gesture of appeal. 'I swear this is true, Barbie. I've been in a kind of wilderness of the heart these past nine years. None of the relationships I've had ever felt really important or vital to me. Then, just a week ago…'

He moved back to her, slowly, his hands lightly curling around her shoulders, his eyes darkly watchful, seeking, wanting to know her heart. '…I met a fairy princess,' he continued gruffly. 'And when she kissed me, it was like magic pouring through my whole body.'

'Mine, too, Nick,' she whispered. 'That's why I came dressed like this tonight, hoping it could be so again.'

'Barbie…'

He sucked in a quick breath and kissed her, and she responded with all the passionate urgency of wanting everything to be right between them, for the magic to burst forth and dispel the shadows that had plagued both of them. The past didn't matter. Only now mattered. Now with Nick. And the journey they could take from here.

It was so good…feeling him wanting her, feeling free to want him right back, knowing she was as special to him as he was to her, the glorious sense of a long, long wilderness ending at last for both of them.

'I'll do everything I can to earn your trust again. Just give me the chance, Barbie,' he breathed into her ear.

'Hold on to me, Nick. Don't let me go.'

'Never!' he swore. 'Never!'

And he kissed her with that vow on his lips, in his heart, and her own heart pounded in unison with his, swelling with the love that had always been there for him.

'Nick?… Barbie…?' Carole's voice calling.

Nick ended their kiss on a ragged sigh. 'Yes…what?' he answered reluctantly.

'I'm about to bring in the cake for Mum. I want you in here with the rest of us.'

'Be there in a minute,' he promised. He eased back, lifting his hands to gently cup Barbie's face. 'Are you okay with this…facing my family with me?'

'Are you?'

'No problem for me. I'm only too happy to have you at my side and let everyone know it's where I want to be.'

'Then I'm happy with that, too.'

His thumb tenderly fanned her cheek. 'I *will* look after you, Barbie.'

'I do trust you to do that, Nick,' she assured him.

His smile was loaded with joyful relief. 'This is the start of us being really together.'

'Yes,' she agreed, smiling her own joyful relief.

And together they walked back into the house— arm in arm—leaving the darkness behind.

There was no place for darkness in their hearts.

They carried magic with them.

CHAPTER SIXTEEN

'HAPPY days, Nick.' Leon grinned at him as he lifted his glass of champagne. 'And nights.'

Nick grinned back. 'You've got that right.'

They stood outside the marquee on Observatory Hill, taking a short breather from the crowd of family and friends within. Barbie and Sue had gone to 'freshen up' and Nick didn't want to circulate amongst the wedding guests without his bride at his side.

'Right woman, right time, right place,' Leon went on approvingly, then cocked a teasing eyebrow. 'Don't know about the date though. You do realise this is the Ides of March, the day that Julius Caesar fell.'

Nick laughed. 'Big Julie was after the crown of Rome. Me... I'd give up any crown to have Barbie as my wife. This was the first available date we could get to have the wedding here and I wasn't waiting any longer.'

'It's only been four months,' Leon reminded him.

Nick shook his head. He'd been waiting all his life for her.

'Sue keeps muttering you charge like a bull, rushing everything.'

'Well, I don't notice the grass growing much under

your feet, my friend,' Nick tossed back at him. 'That's some emerald Sue is flashing on her engagement finger.'

'I don't aim to lose that lady. But there's a lot to be said for a long courtship. I'm relishing every minute of it.'

'Each to his own, Leon.'

'Can't disagree with that. We're both coming out winners and we're not even thirty-one yet,' Leon declared with immense satisfaction.

Nick laughed at his friend's habit of always crunching numbers. Age had nothing to do with how he felt about Barbie. She lit up his life in so many ways, he could only marvel at how lucky he was she'd taken her vengeance on him on this very hill four months ago—the sweetest revenge, reviving as it had the unique bond between them. It was indeed fitting to have their wedding here, Nick thought, because magic *had* been wrought that night and this would always be a special place to both of them.

'Hey! What are you doing out here?'

They both turned to Danny who was proudly carrying out his role of groomsman to Nick.

'Waiting for our women,' Leon answered. 'They've left us to powder their noses.'

'And very pretty noses they are,' Danny commented, grinning at both men. 'Got to say you guys have won prizes with Barbie and Sue.'

Nick suddenly felt impelled to ask, 'No hard feelings, Danny?'

He looked startled. Comprehension dawned slowly and moved into a quizzical frown. 'Over Barbie?'

'You *were* very stuck on her.'

'Youthful obsession,' Danny dismissed as though it were nothing. 'I've fished in many waters since and I'm sure as hell not ready to settle down.'

That wasn't exactly the point, Nick thought, but didn't want to make an issue of it.

Danny picked up on the doubt and gestured an appeal for understanding. 'Fact is, I'm really glad you two have got together. Wish I hadn't been such a pain about Barbie only having eyes for you back in the old days. I didn't realise I was mucking up something special. But I can see it is now, Nick, really special, and I truly am happy for both of you.' He stepped forward, smiling and offering his hand, 'Peace, brother.'

Nick clasped it warmly. 'Thanks, Danny.'

Barbie and Sue came around the corner of the marquee and spotted the three men together. 'Leon,' Sue called, pointing to the entrance, 'the band is playing a great rock beat. Can we dance?'

'We sure can, babe.'

He thrust his glass of champagne into Danny's hand and rock-and-rolled straight over to Sue, who shimmied seductively, the silvery green bridesmaid's dress emphasising her femininity. Leon swung her into the marquee with great panache, and their pleasure in each other left the other three smiling.

'Do you want to dance, too?' Nick asked as Barbie resumed walking towards him.

'I'd rather steal a few quiet moments with you,' she answered.

'Right!' said Danny, plucking the champagne glass out of Nick's hand. 'A good groomsman knows how to look after the bride's and groom's needs. I shall see that you're left alone.'

And off he marched, pausing only to say to Barbie, 'Best thing Nick's ever done, bringing you into the family. You two really belong together.'

'Thank you, Danny.' She watched him enter the marquee, then looked inquiringly at Nick.

'Just clearing up where he stands. No problem for Danny. He's happy for us,' Nick assured her.

She sighed. 'He only ever was, and is, your brother to me.'

'I know.'

The sense of how very, very lucky he was swelled through him as he watched her come the rest of the way to where he stood waiting for her...so breathtakingly beautiful in her wedding gown, like the fairy princess dress, soft and gauzy, clinging to her curves and glittering with silver bugle beads, and her hair like gleaming silk, rippling down over her shoulders. But what shone out of her eyes was more wondrous to Nick than anything else...the love she held for him in her heart...and the trust he'd won back.

He held out his arms and she walked straight into his embrace, curling her own arms around his neck. 'You're wearing the watch I gave you,' she said, a whimsical question in her eyes. 'I didn't notice it until the speeches and you made a toast to my parents.'

'It felt right to wear it today. I love you, Barbie. There never will be anyone else for me.'

'Nor me,' she murmured. 'You were always the one…the love of my life.'

And that was the most magical thing of all, Nick thought as he kissed her, that she'd still been waiting for him when Fate crossed their paths and gave him the chance to realise that she was the one for him.

The only one.

His wife…his soul mate…the love of his life.

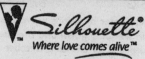

Harlequin truly does make any time special. . . . This year we are celebrating weddings in style!

A Walk Down the Aisle
WEDDING CELEBRATION

To help us celebrate, we want you to tell us how wearing the Harlequin wedding gown will make your wedding day special. As the grand prize, Harlequin will offer one lucky bride the chance to **"Walk Down the Aisle" in the Harlequin wedding gown!**

There's more...

For her honeymoon, she and her groom will spend five nights at the **Hyatt Regency Maui.** As part of this five-night honeymoon at the hotel renowned for its romantic attractions, the couple will enjoy a candlelit dinner for two in Swan Court, a sunset sail on the hotel's catamaran, and duet spa treatments.

A HYATT RESORT AND SPA

Maui • Molokai • Lanai

To enter, please write, in, 250 words or less, how wearing the Harlequin wedding gown will make your wedding day special. The entry will be judged based on its emotionally compelling nature, its originality and creativity, and its sincerity. This contest is open to Canadian and U.S. residents only and to those who are 18 years of age and older. There is no purchase necessary to enter. Void where prohibited. See further contest rules attached. Please send your entry to:

Walk Down the Aisle Contest

In Canada	In U.S.A.
P.O. Box 637	P.O. Box 9076
Fort Erie, Ontario	3010 Walden Ave.
L2A 5X3	Buffalo, NY 14269-9076

You can also enter by visiting www.eHarlequin.com
Win the Harlequin wedding gown and the vacation of a lifetime!
The deadline for entries is October 1, 2001.

HARLEQUIN®
Makes any time special ®

PHWDACONT1

HARLEQUIN WALK DOWN THE AISLE TO MAUI CONTEST 1197
OFFICIAL RULES
NO PURCHASE NECESSARY TO ENTER

1. To enter, follow directions published in the offer to which you are responding. Contest begins April 2, 2001, and ends on October 1, 2001. Method of entry may vary. Mailed entries must be postmarked by October 1, 2001, and received by October 8, 2001.

2. Contest entry may be, at times, presented via the Internet, but will be restricted solely to residents of certain geographic areas that are disclosed on the Web site. To enter via the Internet, if permissible, access the Harlequin Web site (www.eHarlequin.com) and follow the directions displayed online. Online entries must be received by 11:59 p.m. E.S.T. on October 1, 2001.

   In lieu of submitting an entry online, enter by mail by hand-printing (or typing) on an 8½" x 11" plain piece of paper, your name, address (including zip code), Contest number/name and in 250 words or fewer, why winning a Harlequin wedding dress would make your wedding day special. Mail via first-class mail to: Harlequin Walk Down the Aisle Contest 1197, (in the U.S.) P.O. Box 9076, 3010 Walden Avenue, Buffalo, NY 14269-9076, (in Canada) P.O. Box 637, Fort Erie, Ontario L2A 5X3, Canada.

   Limit one entry per person, household address and e-mail address. Online and/or mailed entries received from persons residing in geographic areas in which Internet entry is not permissible will be disqualified.

3. Contests will be judged by a panel of members of the Harlequin editorial, marketing and public relations staff based on the following criteria:

   • Originality and Creativity—50%
   • Emotionally Compelling—25%
   • Sincerity—25%

   In the event of a tie, duplicate prizes will be awarded. Decisions of the judges are final.

4. All entries become the property of Torstar Corp. and will not be returned. No responsibility is assumed for lost, late, illegible, incomplete, inaccurate, nondelivered or misdirected mail or misdirected e-mail, for technical, hardware or software failures of any kind, lost or unavailable network connections, or failed, incomplete, garbled or delayed computer transmission or any human error which may occur in the receipt or processing of the entries in this Contest.

5. Contest open only to residents of the U.S. (except Puerto Rico) and Canada, who are 18 years of age or older, and is void wherever prohibited by law; all applicable laws and regulations apply. Any litigation within the Province of Quebec respecting the conduct or organization of a publicity contest may be submitted to the Régie des alcools, des courses et des jeux for a ruling. Any litigation respecting the awarding of a prize may be submitted to the Régie des alcools, des courses et des jeux only for the purpose of helping the parties reach a settlement. Employees and immediate family members of Torstar Corp. and D. L. Blair, Inc., their affiliates, subsidiaries and all other agencies, entities and persons connected with the use, marketing or conduct of this Contest are not eligible to enter. Taxes on prizes are the sole responsibility of winners. Acceptance of any prize offered constitutes permission to use winner's name, photograph or other likeness for the purposes of advertising, trade and promotion on behalf of Torstar Corp., its affiliates and subsidiaries without further compensation to the winner, unless prohibited by law.

6. Winners will be determined no later than November 15, 2001, and will be notified by mail. Winners will be required to sign and return an Affidavit of Eligibility form within 15 days after winner notification. Noncompliance within that time period may result in disqualification and an alternative winner may be selected. Winners of trip must execute a Release of Liability prior to ticketing and must possess required travel documents (e.g. passport, photo ID) where applicable. Trip must be completed by November 2002. No substitution of prize permitted by winner. Torstar Corp. and D. L. Blair, Inc., their parents, affiliates, and subsidiaries are not responsible for errors in printing or electronic presentation of Contest, entries and/or game pieces. In the event of printing or other errors which may result in unintended prize values or duplication of prizes, all affected game pieces or entries shall be null and void. If for any reason the Internet portion of the Contest is not capable of running as planned, including infection by computer virus, bugs, tampering, unauthorized intervention, fraud, technical failures, or any other causes beyond the control of Torstar Corp. which corrupt or affect the administration, secrecy, fairness, integrity or proper conduct of the Contest, Torstar Corp. reserves the right, at its sole discretion, to disqualify any individual who tampers with the entry process and to cancel, terminate, modify or suspend the Contest or the Internet portion thereof. In the event of a dispute regarding an online entry, the entry will be deemed submitted by the authorized holder of the e-mail account submitted at the time of entry. Authorized account holder is defined as the natural person who is assigned to an e-mail address by an Internet access provider, online service provider or other organization that is responsible for arranging e-mail address for the domain associated with the submitted e-mail address. **Purchase or acceptance of a product offer does not improve your chances of winning.**

7. Prizes: (1) Grand Prize—A Harlequin wedding dress (approximate retail value: $3,500) and a 5-night/6-day honeymoon trip to Maui, HI, including round-trip air transportation provided by Maui Visitors Bureau from Los Angeles International Airport (winner is responsible for transportation to and from Los Angeles International Airport) and a Harlequin Romance Package, including hotel accomodations (double occupancy) at the Hyatt Regency Maui Resort and Spa, dinner for (2) two at Swan Court, a sunset sail on Kiele V and a spa treatment for the winner (approximate retail value: $4,000); (5) Five runner-up prizes of a $1000 gift certificate to selected retail outlets to be determined by Sponsor (retail value $1000 ea.). Prizes consist of only those items listed as part of the prize. Limit one prize per person. All prizes are valued in U.S. currency.

8. For a list of winners (available after December 17, 2001) send a self-addressed, stamped envelope to: Harlequin Walk Down the Aisle Contest 1197 Winners, P.O. Box 4200 Blair, NE 68009-4200 or you may access the www.eHarlequin.com Web site through January 15, 2002.

Contest sponsored by Torstar Corp., P.O. Box 9042, Buffalo, NY 14269-9042, U.S.A.

PHWDACONT2

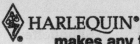

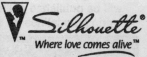